THE NIGHT S
ABOUT

Tears suddenly
She couldn't expect anyone else at the Winter Carnival Ball to share or understand her sheer happiness at this moment. Standing in the limelight with Dex Grantham by her side and a bouquet of flowers in her hand made Gina feel more a part of Midvale High than she had ever felt before. For once, she didn't suffer the slightest tinge of doubt. She belonged.

When the photographers were finished, the escorts led the Court onto the dance floor. As Gina nestled her head against Dex's warm chest, she knew she wouldn't need pictures to remember this evening. The Winter Carnival Ball would live in her memories forever.

Though she didn't know it now, because of this wonderful night Gina would later have to make the hardest decision of her life.

ALL-AMERICAN GIRL

Suzanne Rand

BANTAM BOOKS
TORONTO • NEW YORK • LONDON • SYDNEY • AUCKLAND

RL 7, IL age 12 and up

ALL-AMERICAN GIRL
A Bantam Book / August 1986

Sweet Dreams and its associated logo are trademarks of Bantam Books, Inc. Registered in U.S. Patent and Trademark Office and elsewhere.

Winners is a trademark of Cloverdale Press Inc.

All rights reserved.
Copyright © 1986 by Suzanne Rand and Cloverdale Press Inc.
Cover photo copyright © 1986 by Loren Haynes.
This book may not be reproduced in whole or in part, by mimeograph or any other means, without permission.
For information address: Bantam Books, Inc.

ISBN 0-553-17262-X

Published simultaneously in the United States and Canada

Bantam Books are published by Bantam Books, Inc. Its trademark, consisting of the words "Bantam Books" and the portrayal of a rooster, is registered in U.S. Patent and Trademark Office and in other countries. Marca Registrada. Bantam Books, Inc., 666 Fifth Avenue, New York, New York 10103.

Printed and bound in Great Britain by Hunt Barnard Printing Ltd.

O 0 9 8 7 6 5 4 3 2 1

Her sleek black hair and dark, flashing eyes make blond seem bland. . . . Italy's gift to Midvale High School's cheering squad is tops on the dance floor and hopes to teach others at her own studio one day. . . . Next stop is college and a science major. . . . A burger and fries make her happy. . . . Call her Sophia and make her mad. . . . Gina is proof you don't have to be born here to be the ideal all-American girl.

Entry under Gina Damone's senior picture in *Midvale Memories*, the high-school yearbook.

ONE

Gina Damone could feel her classmates growing restless in anticipation of the final bell. She felt sorry for Mr. McNulty. It couldn't be much fun teaching a last-period class, not when every student at Midvale High was just waiting for the loud *brrring, brrring* that signaled freedom.

Not that Gina was concentrating more intensely than anyone else. For the past ten minutes she'd been busy sneaking peeks at Dex Grantham. Even though he sat on the far side of the room, Gina could see that the attentive look on his handsome face was directed not at their European history teacher, but at the magazine stuck inside his notebook. From the pictures she could see as Dex flipped the pages, Gina guessed it was the latest issue of *Tennis*.

Even sprawled in the regulation school

chair, Dex Grantham's long, lean body was taut as a cat's. The fabric of his shirt strained across the curves of his muscular arms. A wisp of dark hair had strayed across his forehead, and as he shifted position and raised a hand to push it back into place, Gina quickly looked toward her page of notes. If Dex caught her watching him, she'd be horrified.

Up front, Mr. McNulty was droning on, unaware that any of the students gathered before him might be finding his lecture less than mesmerizing.

"While it's true that royalty ignored the impending doom until it was too late, it's generally held to be a fanciful notion that Marie Antoinette actually said of the starving peasants, 'Let them eat cake.' In all probability, her words were—"

As the clanging of the bell cut him off and the students jumped to their feet almost as one, Mr. McNulty blinked his watery blue eyes in surprise. Gina bit her lip to keep from giggling. Even though it happened five times a week, he was always startled when class ended. Gina had heard others call him boring, but she didn't agree. She thought he was adorable; his absent-mindedness was part of his charm.

As the class filed toward the door, Mr.

McNulty said dryly, "We'll have to wait until tomorrow's class to learn what it was the fair Marie actually may or may not have intoned. I hope you'll all survive the suspense."

How can anyone find this wonderful man boring? Gina wondered as she gathered her books. As if in answer to her unspoken question, the affected nasal voice of Valerie Masters, who sat behind Gina, grated against her eardrums.

"Unless Marie said 'School's out,' I can live without knowing," Midvale's head majorette drawled. "How can you sit there every day without twitching around, Gina? You don't *like* this class, do you?" She tittered, as if liking Mr. McNulty's teaching were equal to liking liver and onions.

"I just sit as still as possible so he won't ask me a question and find out I haven't been listening," Gina answered lightly. Valerie would label anyone who said she listened to a lecture as a nerd. Since Valerie got good enough grades to maintain her majorette's position, she had to listen at least some of the time, but if she didn't admit it, neither would Gina.

Gina walked toward her locker with Valerie and Val's best friend, Joanie Gregson, who said little but nodded frequently as Val continued to complain about European history. "You stopping over at Nicola's for a Coke, Gina?" Valerie asked as she and Joanie turned down the side hallway toward their lockers.

"Not till later," Gina answered, continuing along the corridor. "Cheering practice today."

Valerie didn't reply; she just raised one hand in a casual wave. Gina wasn't surprised. Stacy Harcourt frequently said that Valerie had never gotten over not making the cheering squad herself. For Valerie, head majorette didn't seem quite good enough.

Being a cheerleader *was* almost the greatest honor of Gina's life. The only thing she valued more was her position as this winter's cocaptain of the squad. Sharing the title was Stacy herself, the most popular girl in the whole school.

Her pulse quickened as she pushed open the door leading to the girls' locker room. In just a few days, Gina would be leading the cheers at her first game as cocaptain. The squad and the school were depending on her to inspire the support the team needed. From this day on, she couldn't afford to be bashful when the others looked to her for instruction and direction.

Gina was the first of the squad to arrive. In the silence of the empty locker room, she gave herself a pep talk before the other girls came in. *You are the cocaptain,* she reminded herself as she changed from her school clothes into the blue gym shorts and gold sweatshirt she wore for practices. *Act like the cocaptain.*

As often as Gina repeated that speech, she just couldn't breeze along with Stacy's self-confidence or bubble over with the enthusiasm of Tess Belding, the third senior of the squad. She was too shy.

In truth, Gina wasn't sure how much leadership the squad or the students really wanted from her. It wasn't as if anyone really had intended to elect Gina captain. Stacy Harcourt should have had the winter semester election all sewn up. She'd won the election for fall varsity captain by herself when the school voted in the previous spring. Gina Damone made the cheering squad every year because she was such a naturally gifted dancer that the students couldn't refuse her a spot.

But Stacy hadn't bargained on one thing, and neither had the rest of Midvale's student body. Stacy had fallen for Nick Cooper and practically ignored everyone else for him. She'd paid the price for giving the other kids the cold shoulder by sharing her captaincy with Gina, even though she and Nick had stopped dating before the election for cheering-squad captain.

Face it, Gina told herself as she hung her

skirt in her locker, *Stacy's loss was your gain.* Not that Stacy hadn't come back more popular than ever. That was Stacy's way—her talent for popularity was far greater than Gina's for dancing. And Stacy managed to stay at the top so *easily.* For Gina Damone, maintaining popularity wasn't so easy.

Gina glared at her skirt and sweater before she shut the door of her locker. Her clothes were drab compared to Stacy's and Tess's. They wore bold blouses, short, bright skirts, cropped jeans, leather boots, big beads, and wide belts. Gina's mother carefully inspected all of her daughter's clothing purchases; Gina knew not to stray from the flowing solid skirts and conservative sweaters her mother approved.

The muffled sound of approaching voices jolted her from her musings. The other cheerleaders were arriving.

Just remember, she told herself as she slammed shut the gray locker door, *you're the cocaptain. Stacy doesn't have to keep on calling all the shots unless you let her.*

"Well, aren't you the early bird?" teased Sherri Callahan, the most vivacious and outspoken of the juniors on the squad. "I got hung up after class or I would have been here early myself. I was hoping we could go over that great double split you did for the competitions."

"Oh, no! We're not adding that to our regular routines, are we?" Tess Belding, a frantic bundle of fluffy purple wool and tousled light brown hair, followed close behind Sherri. She dumped her overstuffed purse on the bench and looked at Gina with panic, her blue eyes wide within their rims of plum liner and deep lavender eye shadow. "It'll take me months to learn something that complicated! You know my two left feet, Gina."

"Don't worry," Gina assured her. "If we do it at all, I think we'll save it for the semifinals. The guys on the basketball team will probably need something jazzy then."

"Speaking of jazzy," Sherri said to Kathy Phillips, who'd entered quietly and was standing by her locker changing, "I've been meaning to tell you all day how neat your new haircut is. I really like it layered like that."

"Yeah. Good move, Kath," Patricia Petersen chimed in from the row of lockers on the other side of the room. "Now you don't look so much like a junior version of Stacy."

"Thanks. I'm glad you like it," Kathy said softly, but not before an awkward silence greeted Patricia's words. Patricia was just five feet tall, but that didn't stop her from having a big mouth. Everyone knew Kathy was sensitive on the subject of her resemblance to Stacy, especially since she was now going with Rich Stinson, Stacy's ex-boyfriend. Gina mentally applauded Kathy as the other girl continued, "I wish I thought I'd look as good as you do with an even shaggier cut, Pixie."

"It's Patricia, remember? I haven't been 'Pixie' since the summer, Kath!"

"Sorry. It just slipped out," Kathy said mildly, but as she turned back toward her locker, Gina saw her smile.

"Wonder where Stacy's got to?" Tess murmured as she pulled on her shorts. "It's not like her to be late to practice."

Gina glanced up at the big clock on the wall. "Well, we can't wait for her for more than five minutes. I'll bet Ms. Bowen's ready for us in the gym."

"I heard Dex hasn't asked anybody to the Carnival Ball yet," Sherri said. "Maybe he's waylaid her in the halls to tell her she's got another chance."

"Dex only took her out three or four times, didn't he?" Patricia asked. "And that was back before Christmas."

"Don't worry about Stacy, Sherri," Tess said

firmly. "The day that girl's got trouble getting a date is the day I start speaking fluent French!"

"Still having trouble *parlez-vous*-ing?" Gina asked, but she didn't really listen to Tess's answer. She just wanted to steer the subject away from the Carnival Ball before someone asked who was taking her.

She just hoped Dex wasn't asking Stacy to the dance. Not that she expected him to ask *her*: Gina Damone would stick out like a sore thumb in the parade of willowy blondes Dex had dated since Gina moved to Midvale in the ninth grade. But she wasn't sure she could conceal her jealousy if Dex began dating Stacy again.

"We'd better get moving." She broke into the others' chatter. "Don't want to get on the wrong side of the coach before the first game of the season."

Just then they heard the door to the corridor whoosh open. "I'm here! Don't start without me!" Stacy called breathlessly.

"Move it, Harcourt!" Tess whooped. "Don't make all of us late, too."

"Sorry, gang!" Stacy rounded the corner of the bank of lockers, already pulling her pale blue angora sweater over her head, sending her mane of tawny, naturally streaked hair cascading like a silken waterfall. "But I'm just so excited I could explode!"

Everyone stood waiting as Stacy tugged on her sweatshirt and sweatpants. Tess finally urged, "Come on, are you going to tell us or not? What's got you so crazed?"

Brooke Shields couldn't have played the scene better, Gina thought. Slowly, Stacy turned to face them, her long lashes half-lowered over her blue eyes, her heart-shaped face tilting up as a breathy little sigh escaped her parted lips. "I've just been invited to the Winter Carnival Ball," she announced, "by . . ." She hesitated, smiling teasingly.

Here it comes, Gina told herself. *Well, I had to hear it sooner or later.*

But she couldn't bear Stacy's drawing it out like this, especially not when Ms. Bowen was waiting in the gym to start practice. "By . . . ?" she prompted.

"By the hottest guy in the whole school!"

Over the groans that answered Stacy's teasing, Gina said, "Dex, right?" She even managed to keep her envy and irritation out of her voice.

Stacy's reaction took her completely by surprise. Instead of saying yes, Stacy tossed back her blond mane and laughed. "Dex? Dex Grantham? Come on, Gina, you know that was over weeks ago!"

"Who, then?" Tess insisted. "Come on, Stace, we've got to start practice."

"My date for the Ball," Stacy said, drawing out each word, "is Jeremy Edwards."

Gina was so weak with relief she just smiled as the other girls shouted their delight and awe. She didn't actually care who Stacy's date was. It was who he *wasn't* that mattered to Gina!

TWO

"Jeremy Edwards," Kathy said as all six girls crossed the locker room to the door leading into the gym. "He's that transfer student from Vermont, isn't he? He's in my fifth-period study hall Tuesdays and Thursdays. I always thought he was real cute."

"*Cute?* He's more than just cute," Stacy insisted. "He's adorable! That sandy hair and the way it sticks up a little on top and then curls around his ears. And his eyes are green—not hazel but absolute, total, genuine green! And those cute freckles across the bridge of his nose!"

"Watch out, world"—Tess winked at Gina—"Stacy's falling in love again!"

"I'm hardly in love with the guy already! Anyhow, it's easy for you to tease, Tess," Stacy retorted with so exaggerated a pout Gina knew she didn't mind all the attention she was getting.

"You've got Dave Prentice wrapped around your little finger, so it's not as if *you* had to worry about not getting asked to the biggest dance of the whole winter."

Patricia snorted. "Give us a break! By next week, half the guys in the senior class would have asked you."

"Todd Solomon *finally* asked me this weekend," Sherri said. "We're double-dating with my brother and Janet."

"I thought you hated going on dates with Dennis," Patricia reminded her. "'My brother the grind,' remember?"

"Dennis is really bearable now that he's seeing Janet. He's not nearly as serious as he used to be. Besides, Todd's on the track team with him and thinks he's terrific. Not to mention that Dad's letting Dennis take the BMW for the night."

"Won't you feel funny parking afterward?" Patricia asked impishly. "I mean, with your own brother making out in the front seat?"

"You think Janet actually *kisses* Dennis?" Sherri asked in mock horror, and everyone giggled.

Gina laughed along with everyone else, but she was glad when they reached the bleachers where Ms. Bowen was waiting, a pile of royal blue and gold pompoms at her feet. She dreaded being asked about *her* carnival date. "He's just the most mysterious guy in the school," she imagined herself saying in imitation of Stacy's hushed tones. "Mr. Nonexistent!"

"What's up, gang?" Ms. Bowen asked. "Did I miss some hot headline in the *Midvale Sentinel?*"

"Just gossiping about the Ball," Tess explained cheerfully. "You'll be chaperoning, won't you?"

Ms. Bowen nodded. "But I've promised myself to fit in a dance or two with my fiancé. Now, we'd better stop wagging our tongues and start shaking a leg, or we'll be here all night."

Gina added her voice to the war whoop the girls let out as they raced to their places on the hardwood floor, but her heart wasn't in it. Even Ms. Bowen had a date for the Ball!

"We might as well start with high kicks," Stacy said, taking the initiative as usual.

This time Gina didn't nod meekly. "I think we should start with back jumps instead," she told her cocaptain. "And we'd better spend fifteen minutes on them since the squad was looking sloppy last practice."

Looking a bit startled, Stacy opened her mouth as if to disagree. Then, to Gina's satisfaction, Stacy nodded. "Good idea," she said. Raising her voice, she announced, "Fifteen minutes of back jumps, everyone!"

"We'll do running in place, windmills, lunges, and jumping jacks for warm-ups first," Gina added loudly, before her courage faded. She was determined to make sure everyone realized there were two captains this semester. "Okay, let's go!"

They went straight to back jumps after warming up. "Keep those feet tucked under, Tess," was Stacy's sole comment during the criticism period afterward. Gina reminded Kathy to keep her back arched until just before her feet hit the ground again.

"Don't forget, it's the arch that makes the back jump look so good," she said. "Why don't we do those high kicks now?" she suggested to Stacy.

"Right," Stacy agreed. "Unless Ms. Bowen has comments on the back jumps."

"Nope. You two covered it all," the coach assured them, and the high-kicks practice began as Gina reminded herself to ask for Ms. Bowen's comments from then on.

After the high kicks, the two captains led the squad in some of the cheers and routines they'd use for the Friday pep rally and the first basketball game. They were standard cheers and song routines—"Get That Point," "On, Mighty Mustangs," "Hey, Hey, Whaddya Say." Both Gina and Stacy concentrated on coaching the juniors since this was their first varsity basketball season.

"Good practice, everyone!" Gina said after they'd finished. "If you need any help with the words of the cheers you didn't do last year, juniors, just listen to Tess. She's got them down pat."

"Yeah, and she's loud and clear, too!" Stacy kidded, rubbing her ears.

"Some people have great jumps, and some of us just know how to scream louder than the rest." Tess grinned.

"You're looking good, gang," Ms. Bowen told them as they put their pompoms back on the pile and got ready to leave. "If the team's as full of spirit as the cheering squad, Midvale's going to rule the courts this year!"

After practice, everyone had the same urge: to get changed, out of school, and into one of the big booths at Nicola's as soon as possible. Stacy led the way in her little blue Honda. Gina went, as usual, in Tess's Volkswagen, with Sherri and Kathy following in Kathy's mom's car and Patricia driving the scruffy hatchback her father had left behind when her parents divorced.

"Can you imagine what anyone who passes us must be thinking?" Tess chuckled as one after another the cars halted for a red light. "A whole caravan of girls putting on makeup in cars! We must look like a chain of traveling beauty parlors!"

"You can tell everyone you drive *lip*stick shift," Gina quipped, tucking her own cosmetic case back into her purse as the light turned green.

Gina laughed at Tess's loud groan. *At least the other girls don't have to take their makeup off again before they go through their front doors,* she thought.

Nicola's had the best pizza in town, and Midvale students had been hanging out there for years. The grubby papered walls were covered with team pictures, one of which showed a group of gawky guys with crew cuts and slicked-back hair holding a sign announcing, "Illinois Basketball Trophy Winners, 1958."

But what everyone loved about Nicola's was what Stacy referred to as its "G.G.Q."—great gossip quotient. Nicola's was one long, wide room, with pizza ovens and a counter at the back and game machines on the side. The whole center was filed with patched banquettes and formica tables. You could sit in any booth at Nicola's and have an unobstructed view of everyone coming in the door.

Stacy was already in a booth when the others filed in. "I ordered sodas," she told them as they were all hanging their coats on the hooks next to the booth.

"I can't stay long," Tess said as she slid into the booth. "My mom says my room better not look like a disaster area by bedtime, or else. And you all know how much straightening up that means."

"Maybe you should get your drink to go, Tess," Sherri teased.

Tess groaned. "It really does look like a disaster area most of the time, doesn't it?"

"Look at the bright side," Stacy said as the waitress brought their sodas on an old metal tray. "Maybe you can apply for federal aid."

"Write to the President and tell him a tornado hit your room one day while you were at school," Gina added.

"Thanks for the suggestions, guys," Tess said sarcastically, "but I think I'll just clean it up. I haven't seen my new turquoise eye shadow since I bought it two weeks ago, and I've got a feeling it's under the pile of clothes on my chair."

"I should get home early myself," Gina admitted, and in another ten minutes she and Tess left the other four girls going over the new words and moves to "On, Mighty Mustangs," which were different for basketball and football seasons.

"Has anyone asked you to the Ball yet?" Tess asked as she steered her little car out of the pizzeria's parking lot.

"What do you mean *yet*?" Gina asked, trying to keep her voice light. "Nobody's asked me, period. And I'm afraid if anyone does, it's going to be some nerd like Dwight Mendham or Arnold Taylor." She sighed. "I suppose I should just ask Tony and get the whole thing over with! But I'd give anything to have a real date and not just go with somebody whose parents are friends of my parents, you know?"

Tess shrugged. "Tony's the guy who took you to our junior prom, right? I thought he was pretty neat."

"Tony's sweet, but . . ." Gina let her voice dwindle off. She couldn't explain to Tess that she longed to date someone like Dex, someone lean and lanky and all-American, instead of Tony Genovese. She liked Tony, but she couldn't think romantically of any of the guys in the close-knit Italian group of which her family was a part.

"Don't give up hope," Tess urged sympathetically. "Look at it this way—since both Dwight and Arnold have asked you out since the semester started, guys must realize you're allowed to date now."

"Then how come nobody worthwhile's asked me out?" Gina challenged. "I'm not *that* awful!"

"You're not awful, and you know it," Tess chided as she passed her own modern house and continued on a few blocks to Marshall Road, a street of older homes. "Before I started seeing Dave, I never knew from one weekend to the next whether or not I'd have a date. It's like I tried telling Stacy after she'd broken up with Rich Stinson and was panicked she'd be a wallflower: lots of guys wouldn't dare to ask a cheerleader for a date because they'd be too scared of getting turned down."

"So how come it's the drips like Dwight and Arnold who get up the nerve to do it? Oh, listen to me." Gina groaned as Tess pulled up to the curb behind Mr. Damone's station wagon. "I sound like Valerie Masters, making cracks like that. I'm just afraid if I go out with someone like that once, that's what I'll be stuck with. Me and the Arnold Taylors of the world, with their pocketfuls of pens and their shirts buttoned all the way up to the neck! Why did I have to be born with parents who wouldn't let me date till senior year?"

"Just wait, Gina. Somebody fantastic will ask you out soon. You've just got to be patient," Tess assured her. In a smaller voice, she added, "In the meantime, be thankful your folks are at least happy together."

"Poor Tess! Here I am feeling sorry for myself, and you're the one whose parents are breaking up! Isn't there any chance they'll just forget the whole thing?"

"Nope, this is definitely it." Tess stared straight ahead, and in the gathering late afternoon dusk, Gina could see the sparkle of unshed tears in her eyes. "My mom filed for divorce over Christmas vacation. Some present, huh?" She laughed shakily. "The worst part is, she says it's too expensive and not very practical for the two of us to rattle around in that big house now that Dad's not living with us anymore. She's putting the house on the market and talking about buying a condo."

"How awful!" Gina sympathized, staring at her own sturdy two-story brick house, its airy, screened side porch shrouded in the canvas tarps her father diligently put up every winter, its front garden carefully pruned and swaddled in burlap sacking by her mother. "But what about your father?" she asked Tess. "Doesn't he want the house?"

Tess shook her head sadly. "He's talking about trying to get a transfer out West. So he's not even sticking around!"

"Maybe he'll change his mind," Gina said hopefully. "I've heard people get all sorts of crazy ideas when they first get divorced."

"Yeah, look at Patricia's parents." Tess chuckled grimly. "At least Dad isn't dating girls not much older than me the way Mr. Petersen is. And Mom's not trying to look sixteen or hanging out at the singles bars like Patricia's mother. At least I've got Dave. I'd probably crack up without him." Tess smiled warmly. "He's one in a million. I'd better get home and clean up my pigsty of a room if I want to get it done before he comes over later to study."

Gina nodded. "And I'd better get the table set before my mom gets home from work. Thanks for the ride, Tess. You're a real lifesaver."

Gina opened the car door and slid out, turning up the collar of her coat against the icy winds that kept Midvale's residents shivering from mid-October to early May.

When she reached the shelter of the front porch she set her ring binder and books on the decorative little bench there, took a mirror and a tissue from her purse, and rubbed off most of her blusher and all her lipstick. Finally, she picked up her books again, inserted the key in the lock, and let herself in. The putt-putt-putting of Tess's loose exhaust pipe had faded around the corner as she stepped into the hallway and called out, "Hi, I'm home!"

THREE

Gina selected her clothes with care Thursday morning. Something had to boost her flagging spirits by Friday's pep rally. The baggy cropped pants she chose looked enough like a skirt to meet her mother's standards for proper schoolwear, especially with the matching tan short jacket Gina wore with the pants. A heavy cotton turtleneck in a deep gold the color of autumn leaves and golden brown boots brought the outfit together.

Gina knew that none of the people who were smiling and greeting her as they took their regular places in homeroom suspected how low she really was.

When Stacy came in, waving cheerfully as she took her seat across the room, Gina was stabbed by a little pang of envy she couldn't hide from herself. How wonderful to be Stacy Harcourt, fair-haired and willowy with skin like peaches and cream, rather than short and sturdy-looking with an undeniably olive complexion. But Stacy didn't even seem to realize how lucky she was. She just took it for granted.

As Gina admired Stacy, she raised one hand to her own sleek dark hair. She remembered that afternoon in summer when Stacy had first suggested how fabulous Gina would look with shorter hair.

Gina, Tess, and Stacy had been sitting in Stacy's airy white bedroom, experimenting with Stacy's enormous store of cosmetics, when Stacy had begun playing with hairstyles. Tiring of swirling her own tawny mane in new arrangements atop her head, she'd turned to Gina.

"Let's see how you'd look with your hair cut," she'd said, narrowing her eyes in imitation of a professional hairdresser.

When she'd finished rolling and pinning Gina's waist-long black tresses, she crossed her arms and stood back to survey her handiwork. "It looks incredible!" she'd trilled with satisfaction. "Don't you think so, Tess?"

Tess, who liked to get a new hairdo about once a month, had been just as enthusiastic.

"You really do look great, Gina," she'd agreed. "Shorter hair would be much more becoming on you. I think a small-boned face like yours gets buried under all that hair."

"Look at yourself! You'll love it."

Following Stacy's order, Gina had turned toward the mirror. She looked really pretty! So much more chic, like the other cheerleaders. "You're right!" she exclaimed. "I just love it!"

"Then it's settled," Stacy had said matter-of-factly. "Hang on while I run downstairs and get the haircutting scissors."

"But—" Gina started to protest, but it was too late. Stacy had already rushed from the room.

"What's wrong?" Tess had asked. "Stacy's really good at this. She's cut my hair a dozen times."

Gina had just sat there as if her larynx were paralyzed. She'd never let anyone, not even her two best friends, know just how old-fashioned her folks were. She couldn't tell them that she was afraid to cut her hair.

Besides, she hadn't really *wanted* to say no. She'd wanted that haircut desperately. So she'd closed her eyes, feeling a bit sicker to her stomach with every click of the scissors, until Stacy had proclaimed *"Voilà!"* and Gina had looked down at the pile of long, dark clumps scattered on the wall-to-wall carpeting.

Her stomach had clenched into a little iron fist at the realization of what she'd done, but when she'd looked at the mirror, all she'd felt was joy. "It's like I'm another person!"

But she still turned down Tess's offer of a ride that morning. She'd needed time to steel herself before facing the scene she knew awaited her at home.

It had been pretty bad. Her father shook his head in shock, while her mother just kept murmuring, "Your beautiful hair, Gina." Her brother watched open-mouthed. She'd escaped punishment at least, but her father had made it clear she might not be so lucky the next time. "Don't go thinking you're the boss of this household the way so many of these American children do," he'd told her sternly. "Your mama and I still make the rules, Gina."

Gina shook herself back into alertness as the bell ended homeroom period. *No,* she thought as she crossed the room to join Stacy and head for the first-period class they had together, *there's no point in being jealous of Stacy. Too many things separate us for me to even hope to compete in Stacy's realm.*

Gina's mood hadn't improved by the time she headed for lunch after fourth period. If anything, it had slumped even lower. She was beginning to consider doing something drastic, so her parents would send her back to Italy to her grandmother, a punishment with which she was occasionally threatened. Then she wouldn't be expected to attend the Ball! A life of feeding the goats at the hillside farm of her Damone grandparents would be a small price to pay to be saved from the embarrassment of having no date for the Winter Carnival Ball.

Gina wrinkled her nose at the thought of a future among the goats. Thank goodness her grandfather had saved so Gina's father could attend the university in Rome. Eventually, Mr. Damone had moved his family to Brooklyn to teach at a college there, ultimately moving to Midvale to take the prestigious post he now held at the nearby state college. If her family hadn't come to America, Gina might have grown up the way her mother did, attending a small rural school. Still, how bad could the farm be for a week or two, just long enough to get out of going to the Ball?

Gina shuddered as she contemplated the alternative. At assembly the next morning, the names of the Queen's Court would be announced. There wasn't much suspense about the names of the Court members: Midvale's six cheerleaders were almost always chosen, along with one other girl. This year, the seventh girl probably would be Valerie Masters.

Last winter, only five cheerleaders were on the Court. Gina hadn't gotten up the nerve to ask her parents to make an exception to their no-dating rule until it was time for the junior prom. She'd told everyone, even Tess and Stacy, that she was going out of town the weekend of the Ball, ashamed to admit her parents were unlikely to let her attend. Not only had she missed the Ball, she'd had to stay in the house all weekend so no one would find out she'd been in Midvale all along.

This year, Gina resolved, *I won't sit at home. I'll just have to ask Tony.*

Gina stopped dead as a frightening prospect struck her. What if Tony was busy that night and couldn't be her escort? Why had she assumed he'd be dying to take her?

She didn't realize she'd come to a halt until somebody barreled into her from behind, knocking her off balance and sending her purse skimming across the hall. "Hey!" she shouted as she went down on one knee and struggled to right herself. "Are you trying to kill someone?"

Not until she'd scrambled to her feet did she see that the person who'd careened into her and sent her sprawling so awkwardly was none other than Dex Grantham.

Dex wasn't fazed. Laughing, he sauntered back across the hall, Gina's tan clutch bag in one hand. "That's how I like to impress girls," he said in a low, sexy voice as he handed her the bag. "I just bowl 'em over."

"Well—well—you should look where you're going!" she sputtered, no longer angry but too flustered by his nearness to drop her pose.

"Right. I should look where I'm going—and you shouldn't stop like that," he said, his tone light and teasing, his eyes twinkling. He flashed his perfectly straight white teeth in a grin. "Your head must have been someplace in the clouds, which is a funny place for it to be when you're only about . . . what, five four?"

She nodded. By then, Dex was standing so

close to her he could easily gauge the difference in their heights.

He raised one arm to prop himself against the wall next to her, so close his soft Shetland sweater brushed her cheek. "Hey, I was thinking, Gina," he began.

She held her breath, not daring to breathe. *Is Dex going to ask me out? Is he actually going to ask me to the Ball?*

"There you are!" The strident, nasal twang of Valerie Masters shattered the intimate scene. "Really, Dex, I've been waiting by your locker for at least five minutes! Didn't you promise you'd run me over to the mall during lunch so I could pick up my shoes? Oh, hi, Gina."

"Hi, Valerie." Gina studied her wristwatch. "I'd better run if I want to grab lunch."

Valerie wrinkled her nose. "Smells like meat loaf. They've got a lot of nerve calling it that, don't they?" She grabbed Dex's arm. "Come on, will you? I've got to be back for sixth period, and I want at least to grab a slice of pizza or something."

"All right already, I'm coming!" he said, but he pushed himself slowly away from the wall. As if Valerie wasn't even there clinging to his arm, he gave Gina a slow, lazy smile, as if they shared some delicious secret. "I'll talk to you in history."

"Sure," Gina agreed weakly as she turned and started to leave. "See you then."

Dex was just up to his usual flirtation, Gina admitted to herself with a sinking heart. She'd been a fool to think he'd been planning to ask her to the Carnival Ball! It was obvious that he'd be taking Valerie. No girl would expect a boy she wasn't dating to run her errands. Those shoes were probably for the dance. *I should have known,* she thought defeatedly. Valerie and Dex were always whispering and fooling around together.

Face it, Gina scolded herself. *Valerie's his type and you're not with a capital "N."* It was just like the movies: girls like Valerie with long honey-colored hair, icy blue eyes, and features sharp as if they'd been chiseled always got the guy, even if they were petty and scheming, like Val.

Gina had to call Tony as soon as she got home from school. She prayed he wasn't busy that weekend. *It isn't as if there's anything wrong with Tony,* she told herself as she pushed through the double doors and into the lunchroom. *Lots of girls would probably jump at the chance to date Tony. After all, he's handsome, intelligent, and funny.*

There was only one thing really wrong with Tony Genovese besides the fact that Gina's parents would love to see her dating him. He just wasn't Dex Grantham. And that meant he just wasn't enough.

FOUR

The rest of the day couldn't pass quickly enough for Gina. Even as she sat with Tess, Stacy, Janet Perry, and Marsha Steiner at their usual long table in the cafeteria, her thoughts remained centered on Dex. She replayed the scene with him over and over again. Maybe he was just flirting. But maybe he really did want to ask her for a date. When Julie Easton, the senior class president, joined the group at their table, Gina stopped daydreaming just long enough to give her a welcoming smile.

Be serious, Gina, she admonished herself as her thoughts drifted back to her romantic possibilities. *Maybe Dex just wanted to ask if Stacy's got a date yet.*

But no matter what Gina told herself, she was excited all over again every time she remembered his intimate parting smile.

"What do you think, Gina?"

"Huh?" She focused on Julie Easton's questioning glance. "Sorry . . . my mind was wandering."

"I was saying, wasn't it unreasonable of Steve to expect me to ask my dad for the car for the dance next weekend so he could leave *his* at Customcar for a paint job?" Julie was all rationality except when it came to squabbling with her boyfriend.

Out of the corner of her eye, Gina could see the other girls rolling their eyes at one another, but she kept a straight face as she answered Julie. Maybe Julie's worries were silly, but they were important to Julie. The poor girl looked tortured as she stared across the room to where Steve was sitting with Zack Wenner and Mary Bowes.

"Well," Gina said slowly, "I can understand Steve thinking it was unfair of you to count on using his car all the time, but it doesn't seem very fair of him to expect you to ask your dad for the car just because *he* wants it, either."

"I can't believe the two of you made such a big deal out of the whole thing," Stacy interjected. "Come on, Julie, you've been through this enough before. You know the two of you will be kissing and making up before the day's through. It's just a question of who makes the first move."

"You really think it's not all over?" Julie asked eagerly, as if she and Steve didn't have a big blowup every week.

"Uh-huh." Stacy nodded as she pushed away her half-eaten meat loaf. "Unless he's poisoned by today's lunch."

As the other girls giggled, Julie abruptly pushed back her chair and started to rise. "I'm not going to sit here and watch him laughing his head off with Zack and Mary when he doesn't care if I live or—"

She didn't get a chance to finish before Stacy pulled her back down onto the chair. "Hang on a minute. I think he's coming over here!"

Sure enough, Midvale's star forward shuffled over until he stood behind Julie's chair, then ducked his head and mumbled, "Do you think we could go out in the hall and talk for a minute?"

"Oh, I suppose so," Julie consented reluctantly as she rose and followed him out of the lunchroom.

"Well, it looks like the cold war's off." Stacy chuckled.

"If Dave and I ever start bickering like those

two, kick me, will you somebody?" Tess remarked.

Girls like Julie don't know how silly they are, Gina thought. *I'd never take a guy so lightly or risk his love so impulsively.*

At the moment she would have settled for just a date. A real boyfriend was starting to seem like too much to hope for.

Gina restlessly endured her next two classes, barely hearing a word or taking a note. But as she entered the classroom for European history, Gina's heart raced. She was careful not to study Dex as he slouched at his desk on the other side of the room. In his reedy voice, Mr. McNulty began discussing the political climate of Europe in the eighteenth century. Gina always took a few notes on McNulty's lectures, but this afternoon she was so intent on concentrating on the teacher, not Dex, that she filled three pages, front and back.

She didn't rush out when the bell rang announcing the end of the school day. What if she ended up dawdling in the corridor and Dex strolled right by her without a word? She poked around in her looseleaf binder, making a show of putting her notes in order. But Dex wasn't hurrying to join her. She could hear him—still at his desk—talking about a party at his brother's college fraternity house the weekend before. Finally, her body rigid with irritation, she snatched up her books and left the room. She should have known Dex didn't really want to talk to her. He'd just been trying to needle Valerie or make her jealous.

"Gina, wait up! Where are you going?"

She'd no sooner rounded the corner into the corridor when Dex caught up to her. "Hey, I told you I wanted to talk to you after class, didn't I?"

"I figured if you had something to say, you'd find me," she replied with a flippancy that surprised her.

"Well, here I am!" he retorted. "You heading over to Nicola's?"

"Not today. I told Tess to go without me. My mom's got a, um, a meeting tonight, so I've got to get right home to help with dinner. I'm going to catch the bus."

"You don't have to do that," Dex told her. "Come on, get your stuff out of your locker and I'll give you a ride. Meet me by the parking lot door, okay?"

"Sure," she said readily, but she was more puzzled than ever. Dex Grantham, who'd never gone out of his way to be more than casually friendly, suddenly had offered her a ride. He wanted something. Gina battled her rising hopes.

If Dex asked what kind of meeting her mother had, she'd say the garden club. Stacy Harcourt's mother belonged to the garden club. Gina hadn't told anyone that her mom went to night school to work on a high school diploma. Nor would she admit that her mom took the bus to and from her job as a computer operator at Adler Aeronautics because she'd never learned to drive. Her friends would think the Damones were really from the Dark Ages.

Dex waited by the exit for her. He bounced one hip against the door to open it for her, saying, "You live over by the Beldings, don't you?"

Gina nodded. "Marshall Road." It had never occurred to her that Dex might know where she lived.

"It always feels great to leave old man McNulty's class, doesn't it? He puts me to sleep the way he drones on. How a guy can get so turned on by things that happened hundreds of years ago beats me. I'll take a guy like Mr. Dempsey any day."

"Dempsey's a lot hipper, that's for sure," Gina agreed. She wasn't crazy about the young biology instructor she'd had last year. Mr.

Dempsey was too busy trying to act like one of the gang to be much of a teacher. "Mr. Partridge is the worst, though."

Dex stopped by his sleek silver sports car and reached into a pocket for the keys. "Are you taking chem with Partridge?" he asked as he unlocked the passenger door and held it open for her. "He's the pits. I hear he actually makes fun of kids who get the answers wrong on equations."

"Aren't you taking chemistry?" Gina asked as Dex got into the driver's seat.

"I don't have any choice, not if I'm going to major in premed. But I got my dad to pull a few strings with an old buddy of his on the school board so I'd get Evans instead of Partridge. All old Mrs. Evans cares about is making sure everybody passes." He chuckled as he turned the key and started revving up the engine. "That's my kind of teacher."

"This car's gorgeous," Gina said as he zoomed out of the parking lot. When he took the corner with a loud squeal of tires, she thought about reaching over to fasten her seat belt, then decided against it.

"Yeah, this baby can really move," he shouted happily over the noise of the exhaust. "My father gave it to me for my last birthday, after he'd been made head of surgery at the med center. Guess he decided it wasn't dignified enough for the chief surgeon. I'd rather have this than his Mercedes any day. I like knowing I'm in a car, you know?"

It would be pretty hard to forget I'm in this car, Gina thought as Dex accelerated into a curve and she was flung hard against the car door.

"Speaking of teachers, my brother's majoring in engineering and he's got your old man for a course this year. Says he's something else. Nobody misses Professor Damone's lectures, according to him."

"I didn't know your brother was going to be an engineer," she commented, avoiding the topic of her father. She'd visited a few of his classes and knew why nobody missed his lectures. Her father was prime-time entertainment, laughing and shouting and teaching engineering as if he were auditioning for a Shakespearean comedy. College professors were expected to have class, Gina knew. They weren't supposed to make fools of themselves in front of the students the way her dad did. They called him eccentric, but Gina knew what they really meant was that he was a joke.

"Yeah. Crazy, huh? He'll never make half what he would as a doctor."

"My house is two blocks up on the right," Gina said, wondering if she had imagined any hint from Dex that he wanted to talk to her about something.

He didn't ease into it. Pulling up to the curb with a squeal of brakes, he turned to her and asked, "So, you want to go to the Winter Carnival Ball with me?"

The question was such a shock that Gina spoke without thinking. "You mean you're not going with Valerie?" she asked.

"Masters?" He shook his head. "Nah, she's all hung up on this college freshman. Thinks he's a big deal just because he's a year older than us. You should have seen her over at the mall today, running from store to store. 'Do you really like these shoes, Dex? Don't I look fantastic in this dress? I wish you'd answer me, Dex. I only asked you to come so I could get a man's opinion!'" His imitation of Valerie's imperious tones was so accurate that Gina had to giggle.

"I guess she knows she's sure to be named to the Court tomorrow."

"So are you, right? What do you say? You already have a date or do you want to go?" he asked impatiently.

"Oh, I—" She bit her tongue before she

ended up sounding too eager. "I don't have anything *definite*," she told him, saying a silent prayer of thanks that she hadn't already asked Tony. "I'd like to go, sure. That'll be great."

"Okay then. It's a date. You going to Marsha's party after the game Saturday night?"

"No, I can't," she said. That was the night her folks and their Italian friends would be getting together at the Genoveses' house. Gina would have preferred going to Marsha's, but she hadn't dared to ask. "I've got other plans," she added, hoping Dex would think she meant a date.

He shrugged. "I guess I won't see you there, then. I'll probably end up going to this blowout at my brother's frat house, anyhow." He turned the key in the ignition, and the engine roared into life again. "Catch you later," he said as Gina grabbed her books and scrambled out of the car.

Gina floated up the path to the door. It had happened, it had really happened! Dex Grantham had asked her for a date. And not just any date, either. He'd asked her to the Winter Carnival Ball!

As she drifted toward the house, she dug into one pocket for a tissue and automatically buffed her lips and cheeks. She couldn't risk punishment now, of all times. Gina smiled to think that only that morning she'd wished to be banished to Italy. She shook her head in wonder, grinning at her reflection in the glass storm door as she reached for it. Italy was no place for her, not for Dex Grantham's date!

FIVE

"I'm in the kitchen, Gina!" Elio Damone's deep bass voice boomed as Gina closed the door behind her.

Her father was standing in front of the stove when Gina entered the room, stirring a pungent mixture in a huge pot. He looked even less like a professor than usual with the red-and-white "Kiss the Cook" apron Dino had given him for Christmas tied around his fleshy middle.

"Better set the table right away, Gina," he said, the words heavily accented. "Your mama should be home any minute if her bus was on time."

"Sure, Dad," she told him. "I'll just change into my jeans first. Something sure smells good! What is it?"

"Chicken cacciatore. With Elio Damone's added specialty, hot garlic sausage. When you're upstairs, tell your brother to wash up and get down here, all right? He can finish his homework after we eat."

Gina took the stairs two at a time, eager to change. Her parents didn't consider jeans proper for school, and she wore them only around the house and on an occasional weekend. As she passed her brother's door, she knocked loudly and stuck her head in.

"Hi, Gina. Time to eat?" Nine-year-old Dino looked up from where he lay on one of his twin beds reading a dog-eared issue of *Tiger Beat*.

"Almost. Dad says to wash up. Mama's got school tonight, you know. He thinks you're up here working on *homework*," she added.

Dino grinned, and Gina smiled as she closed the door and continued on past the bathroom to her own room.

The odor of garlic overwhelmed Gina as she opened the dining room hutch and started removing the ironstone dishes to set the table. She'd have to talk her mother into planning a less pungent meal for the night of the Ball. The smell was enough to knock out two people in the cramped interior of Dex's little car.

Gina sighed, listening to her father puttering around in the next room, talking out loud in

Italian as he cooked. If only her father were more like Alexander Harcourt, who was well groomed and dignified and looked more like an ambassador than an attorney. Her own father had been in America more than seven years, and he still wouldn't stop wearing those awful suspenders. Gina had been a little girl in Brooklyn when she realized that American men wore belts with their trousers. When she'd asked her father why he didn't, he'd been puzzled. "Why wear a belt when suspenders are more comfortable?" he'd asked, and that question was closed.

He had a Ph.D., so it wasn't as if he was too dumb to know he didn't fit in with his suspenders and baggy suits, his loud laugh and broad gestures, his irritating habit of using Italian expressions when American ones would do.

Her mother was no better, with dowdy dresses that hid her figure and sleek black hair twisted into a bun. She had a beautiful face, but Gina thought her mother would look more modern if she wore makeup in addition to her usual touch of lipstick.

If only my mom would wear tailored skirts and silk blouses like Mrs. Harcourt, or jeans and tennis shoes like Tess's mother, she'd look terrific. She'd look like any other Midwestern mother. Gina sighed again. Her mother would stick out as a fashion misfit in a crowd of Midvale moms.

As if she'd conjured her mother up, Gina heard the slam of the front door that signaled Mrs. Damone's entrance. A few seconds later, her mother walked into the dining room. Her face was bright from the cold, and she looked young in spite of her shapeless brown knit dress.

"You have the table set already?" she asked. "*Bene!* What a good girl, Gina. I'll go help your papa, and we will eat in just a few minutes." Gina felt a quick flash of love for her mother. She tried so hard, and she was so proud of her son and her daughter.

As he spooned grated Parmesan onto his fragrant chicken, Gina's father remarked, "So this Saturday you lead the cheering team at the first basketball game since you became captain?"

She nodded. "Only it's called a squad, and I'm not captain. I'm cocaptain."

"You know, Elio, maybe we should miss seeing the Genoveses and go to Gina's game this once," her mother suggested.

"No, Mama, you don't have to do that," Gina said quickly. "None of the other girls' parents come to the games, just basketball fans."

Across the table, Dino's brown eyes regarded her curiously. Of course he knew lots of other Midvale parents attended the games, Gina realized, looking back down at her plate.

"You're sure you don't mind that we never come to see you cheer?" her mother asked doubtfully.

"No, honest. I'd probably have a hard time concentrating if you ever came. I'd be too busy worrying what you thought," Gina explained. In truth, she knew she'd be more worried about what the other kids would think of her parents. "Besides," she added, "I was really looking forward to seeing the Genoveses this week."

There goes any chance you had of going to Marsha's party, she told herself as her mother's face brightened noticeably. Not that it really mattered. When she did go to Midvale parties Gina never stayed long, always arriving with an excuse for leaving early. She couldn't confess that her parents thought eleven o'clock was a lenient curfew for a high school senior.

"I know Tony and little Maria will be glad to see you," Mrs. Damone said. "And I think the DiPietro girls will be there, too."

Gina nodded. She couldn't get too excited about the thirteen-year-old DiPietro twins, chubby girls who spent most of their time giggling and gorging themselves on cookies. And six-year-old Maria Genovese was too young to do much besides play checkers with Dino.

Gina did enjoy the time she spent with Tony. He didn't intimidate her the way so many of the boys at Midvale did. And in spite of being a high scorer on his school's soccer team and a class officer, Tony wasn't stuck on himself.

Romantically speaking, however, Tony wasn't Gina's type. He wasn't even in Dex's league. But very few boys were.

"Oh, by the way, Mama and Dad," Gina said, emerging from her reverie. "Our big Winter Carnival Ball is weekend after next, so I'll be tied up that Saturday night."

"A school dance?" her mother murmured.

"It's a formal," Gina explained. "I'll need a dress. But I've got some money saved up I can put toward it," she added quickly, before either of her folks could say no. "Tomorrow at school they announce the names of the Queen's Court, and it seems like I'll be one of them."

"The Queen's Court? You mean you were

picked out of all the girls to be on it?" Gina was sure the neighbors could hear her father's enthusiastic roar.

Gina nodded. "Only seven girls are picked by the whole student body, Dad, so it's a pretty big deal."

"Congratulations, *bellissima!*" her father said as her mother beamed with pleasure.

"Will you ask Tony to escort you again?" her mother asked, obviously remembering last year's prom.

"No, I've got another date, Dex Grantham. He's Dr. Grantham's son."

"I have his brother for a class," her father said. "I suppose it's his brother. Mark Grantham . . . his father is a surgeon at the medical center, I believe."

"That's right."

Slowly, Mr. Damone nodded. "I see no reason why you shouldn't attend your Carnival Ball with Dex." His eyes crinkled as a smile replaced his serious expression, and he added, "And we can't expect you to wear last year's prom dress, can we? What do you think, Magdalena?"

"Of course you may go, Gina. And you can have a new dress, too."

"Oh, thank you! Maybe I can go over to the mall on Saturday morning to look at dresses. Can I use the car then, Dad?"

"I don't see why not," her father agreed.

"I'll come with you, Gina," her mother interjected. "We can shop for your dress together."

"Great," Gina said, but her excitement faded. Her mother's idea of a nice dress was bound to be something fit for a grammar school recital. At least they'd said she could go.

"Did I tell you a letter came today from your cousin Giuliana?" Mr. Damone asked his wife.

Her mother registered dismay at her husband's words. "A letter from Giuliana and you didn't let me know? Where is it? Have you read it?"

Pushing back his plate, Gina's father left the room to get the unopened letter, and the remainder of the meal was spent discussing Cousin Giuliana and news of Sicily. Gina listened in amusement as her brother plied her parents with questions. "How old is Cousin Giuliana's son Carlo? Does he go to school in Sicily? If we go to visit, could we stay with them?"

As far as Gina was concerned, Italy was a beautiful country and would always be her native land, but it was in the past. The present was Midvale and cheerleading and Dex Grantham and the Winter Carnival Ball. She would just have to whisk Dex in and out of the house and through introductions before he could see how foreign her parents still were.

SIX

"Nervous about the assembly?" Tess asked as she and Gina headed toward school in her little car.

"A little," Gina admitted. "Everyone keeps saying all the cheerleaders get picked for the Court each year, but every once in a while I find myself wondering, what if this year's different?"

"Me, too," Tess agreed, to Gina's surprise. Of course Tess would be chosen. "But I suppose we'd be pretty conceited if we were too sure of ourselves. I heard Vicious Val's got some college guy lined up as a date and splurged on a dress that's just *tooooo* fabulous." She giggled. "And Stacy was going to the mall last night armed with her mom's charge card to pick up a blue strapless she found at the Brigitte Shop. I'm stuck with my old lilac satin, since Mom says there's no way we can afford to get me a new dress."

"That dress looks so nice on you, though, Tess. It really does."

"Thanks. But you don't have to try to cheer me up about showing up in the same old thing. I read this terrific article on redoing formals, so I'm going to make mine over. I'll bet nobody will even recognize it!"

"Do it over?" Gina asked doubtfully, remembering a few of Tess's other fashion makeovers that had turned out disastrously.

"Oh, don't worry, I'm not going to cut it or dye it or do anything drastic. Not like the time I tried to turn that awful red cotton jumper into a batik sundress. Remember, in tenth grade?"

Gina laughed. "How could I forget?"

"Well, how was I supposed to know it was going to end up looking like I had a bull's–eye on my behind?" Tess feigned indignation. "Just wait, this ball dress will be dynamite."

"I'm going out to the mall with my mom tomorrow to look for something."

"Lucky you! Did you call Tony?"

"Oh, I didn't have to, after all." Gina aimed for just the right offhand tone. "Dex asked me to go with him."

"Dex Grantham?" Briefly, Tess took her eyes

off the road and looked at Gina with an expression the other girl couldn't comprehend. "You're going to the Winter Carnival Ball with Dex?"

"You sound surprised," Gina remarked, puzzled by her friend's lack of enthusiasm.

Tess shrugged. "I never would have thought he was your type, that's all."

"We're just going to the dance together, not eloping," Gina said lightly. But Gina knew it wasn't that Tess thought Dex wasn't Gina's type—Tess was amazed that Dex had asked Gina.

"Oh, I think it's great!" Tess insisted. "He's probably about the only guy in school who could keep up with you on the dance floor." She hesitated, then changed the subject. "How come you stopped taking dance lessons, Gina?"

Gina laughed. "One day last year I woke up and decided, why keep torturing myself?"

"You mean dancing's that hard?"

"No." Gina sighed. "Dancing's a breeze. I mean, it's like eating and sleeping for me. But what was the point in knocking myself out taking the bus all the way across town twice a week for studio classes when it would never come to anything? You don't know my folks, Tess. They'd never let me major in dance in college. Not in a million years. The way they see it, only science and math are important subjects."

"Oh, Gina, how awful! Have you tried to talk to them about it?"

Gina shook her head. "It wouldn't do any good. They're—well, set in their ways, I guess you could say. Besides, I was busy cheering and was having trouble fitting the lessons in."

"But to completely drop it like that—" Tess's voice faded as she turned in to the school parking lot.

"It doesn't really bother me anymore," Gina insisted. She'd already told Tess more than she'd meant to. Gina couldn't admit to anyone, not even a caring and understanding friend like Tess, how different her parents were from other people's parents. "Are you going to Marsha's party tomorrow night?" she asked.

"Yeah. I'm meeting Dave there, since he'll be going to the game in his own car. I can give you a ride to Marsha's if you want," she added as she slid the car into a space and flicked off the ignition.

"Thanks a lot," Gina told her as she swiveled out, locking the door behind her. "But I'm not going."

"How come? Marsha's parties are the greatest—nobody misses them. There's always enough food to feed the entire senior class at her house! I can't believe you're not going!"

Gina hugged her books to her chest as the two girls walked up the path to the three-story building. For an instant, she was tempted to confess to Tess that she hated to go to parties since she always had to be the first to leave.

But senior year was half over. She'd managed high school so far without anyone finding out how strict her parents were. She had told her friends she wasn't allowed to date until senior year. But as much as possible, she tried to pretend she had the same privileges as her friends but was just too busy to go to every party. This wasn't the time to tell Tess about curfews.

As Gina crossed through the side entrance and hurried down the hallway, she was greeted by almost everyone she passed, even sophomores and juniors whose names she didn't know. On this pep rally day, even people who might not have recognized her otherwise knew who she was by her distinctive Midvale cheerleader's blue and gold outfit.

Assembly replaced the morning's first period. After homeroom ended, Stacy nudged Gina all the way down the hall to the auditorium. "Hurry, Gina," she urged. "We've got to save seats so the whole squad can be sitting together when our names are announced."

"What if not everyone from the squad is chosen?" Gina asked, not willing to admit to Stacy that she worried she might be the one left out.

"Don't be dense! Of course everyone on the squad's going to be on the Court. Everybody knows that, Gina. Now, come on, let's hustle."

In spite of her anxiety, Gina was amused. "Don't you ever worry about *anything*, Stacy?" she asked as they maneuvered around other students and down the aisle of the auditorium.

"Of course I do, Gina," Stacy answered blithely. "I worry about a lot of things. Believe me, I was really worried after getting involved with Nick Cooper and all that. For a while, I was afraid I'd end up really unpopular. But that turned out okay, didn't it? So it didn't matter much whether I worried or not." She shrugged. "We should probably sit here in the third row, don't you think? The first row might look too pushy."

"I think this is fine," Gina assured her, filing into the middle of the row. "Of course," she added, "you don't have to worry about being on the Court. Everybody's sure you'll be Queen."

"Oh, do you really think so, Gina?" Those

beautiful blue eyes were so wide that if Gina didn't know better, she'd have thought Stacy hadn't even considered ruling over the Court until that moment. "I hope I do get it. I remember last year how much I wished I could change places with Ellen McGee when they crowned her and all the flashbulbs started popping. Look, there's Sherri and Kathy. Wave, so they won't miss us."

Gina suppressed a grin as Stacy started waving with every inch of her body. "Oh, good, they see us," Stacy said. "And here come Patricia and Tess. Look, Gina, over there. See Nick Cooper smiling at me? I wonder if he's all that happy with his new girlfriend."

"You're not still hung up on him, are you?" Gina asked in surprise as she and Stacy sank back into their seats again.

"Not really. He's just so darned cute! But you can't imagine what it's like to be with somebody who's just not your type, Gina. Let's face it, looks don't go very far when the two of you have nothing to talk about. And Nick and I had nothing in common, absolutely zip, zero, zilch. Not like me and Jeremy." She sighed happily. "We can talk for hours!"

The dreamy look in her eyes vanished as the other cheerleaders clambered into the row.

Just before the lights dimmed, Stacy turned to Gina and asked, "Who's taking you to the Ball, anyway? I've been so busy bragging about Jeremy I forgot to ask you."

"I'm going with Dex," Gina told her, amazed at how easily those words were starting to roll off her tongue.

"So he'll get to have a date on the Court, after all!" Stacy smiled. "Oh, I don't mean I think that's why he asked you," she added quickly. "I'm just surprised he got up the nerve to ask anyone with as much class as you've got."

Gina just smiled, but as the auditorium went totally dark, she wished Stacy hadn't brought up something Gina had refused so far to think about: What if Dex Grantham *had* invited her only because every other cheerleader already had a date?

She forced the unwelcome thought from her mind. The important thing was that he had asked. She had a chance to show him just how good she could be for him. Dex had a reputation for playing the field, but that didn't mean the right girl couldn't get him to settle down. Maybe Stacy was jealous that she hadn't been the right girl for Dex.

Stacy was right about one thing, though. When the Queen's Court was named, all six squad members heard their names called and stood, one by one, as the rest of the students applauded them. And as Stacy had predicted, Valerie Masters was the seventh member of the Court.

Tess giggled as Valerie's name was announced. "That's some look on Val's face," she observed. "She's definitely not happy to be standing all alone over there. I only hope she's in a good mood at the Ball."

"She should be," Gina reminded Tess as they sat. "She's going to get to show off her big-deal college boyfriend."

"Yeah, and act like the rest of us are crazy to be dating high school guys," Tess said. "Hey, Stace, did Gina tell you who she's going to the dance with?"

"The divine Dex, you mean?" Stacy turned to Gina. "Actually, you should have a fabulous time. Dex just loves being in the spotlight, you know."

"Who doesn't?" Gina challenged.

"Did I hear you say you're going with Dex Grantham, Gina?" Sherri leaned forward in her seat. "You'll look fantastic in the passenger seat of that Porsche!"

"You two should make a cute couple," Kathy Phillips put in.

"I just hope you don't get seated next to me in the Court," Patricia added impishly. "Dex Grantham's enough to make any other guy look like chopped liver, even Brent."

"Are you going with Brent Halstrom? He's adorable, Patricia!" Gina said warmly. "Really, he's one of the cutest guys in the junior class." For the first time, she felt like a real participant in a conversation about boys and dates.

"Dave said he'd wait for me at the back of the auditorium," Tess said in a low voice as they rose to the tape-recorded strains of "Midvale High School, Hail to Thee." Stacy was already craning around to spot Jeremy.

Gina imagined herself casually saying things like, "Gotta run, Dex is waiting," or, "I guess I won't be at Nicola's after practice today—I'm meeting Dex." *One day it will be like that for me, too,* Gina thought hopefully as the music swelled around her.

SEVEN

"How about this one, Gina? This is very nice," Mrs. Damone commented, holding up a hanger as the two stood in the juniors department of Haynes's department store at the mall.

Gina thought the dress was horrible. She wanted to tell her mother she'd rather stay home for the rest of her life than show up at a Midvale formal wearing this pink dress with its lace-trimmed high neck and ruffled long sleeves. But she knew that wasn't the way to end up with anything she liked.

Gina tried to look as if she were really considering the dress before slowly shaking her head. "I don't think so, Mama. Pink's okay for blonds, but I look absolutely pea green in colors like that. Let's look in the misses department, okay? I can wear an eight as well as a seven."

"Don't you think everything there will be

too old for you?" Mrs. Damone sounded doubtful, but she followed her daughter out of the department and across the store's second floor.

"You really can't go by that anymore," Gina explained. "There's hardly any difference between misses and juniors when it comes to dresses."

"I certainly can't imagine myself in any of *those* outfits," her mother said with a chuckle, nodding toward a display of shoulder-padded big tops, bright accessories, and pegged pants at the front of the misses department.

When Gina was in the center of the department floor, she stopped short and her mother bumped into her. "What's wrong?" Mrs. Damone asked.

"Look at that dress!" Gina clutched her mother's arm, staring wide-eyed at the burgundy velvet dress on the mannequin toward the rear of the department. "Isn't it gorgeous?"

"Beautiful," her mother agreed. "They have so many pretty things here, don't they?"

From her mother's tone, Gina could tell she didn't consider the dress a possibility for the dance. But it was so gorgeous, she just had to try it on. She scanned the racks for a flash of burgundy velvet.

"Oh, look, they're having a sale on knit

dresses," her mother said, nodding at the signs on some racks across the floor. "I could use a new dress for work. It seems I'm always too busy to buy anything but pantyhose. And then I wonder why I have nothing new to wear!"

"Why don't you browse over there while I check out the dressier things?" Gina suggested. "You can meet me over here when you're done."

"I think I'll do that. Just remember, don't bother to look at anything in black."

"Don't worry, I won't," Gina promised.

The burgundy was there among the formal dresses, and in a size eight, too. But Gina knew she'd be wasting time trying to talk her mother into buying that dress. She riffled the row of gowns, but found nothing she knew she and her mother would agree on. A green taffeta caught her eye until she realized the sleeves were meant to be worn off the shoulders and the neckline plunged lower than her mother would ever approve.

Her mother had not returned by the time Gina had eliminated all the dresses on the rack. She found the burgundy dress again. Turning the dress on its hanger so it faced her, she ran her fingers over its plush nap. It was the most beautiful dress she'd ever seen, simple yet feminine, with a heart-shaped neckline, puffy sleeves, and a tulip skirt that blossomed out from a nipped waistline.

"Ah, you found that pretty dress! See anything that would be right for your dance?"

Gina wheeled around as if she'd been caught stealing. "Oh, Mama. That was quick. Didn't you find anything?"

To Gina's surprise, her mother nodded. "I think I need your opinion before I try it on. It may be too—what's the word? sporty?—too sporty for work. We'll stop there on the way out. Now, what have you found?"

Gina took one step back from the dress she was admiring. "This," she said simply. "I love this dress!"

Mrs. Damone lifted the price tag and Gina held her breath. "It is reasonable. But"—she shook her head—"it's such a deep color for a girl. And that neckline—it's almost off the shoulders." Stepping closer to the rack, she pulled out another velvet, a green dirndl with lace collar and cuffs. "What about this one?"

Gina shook her head. "It's pretty. But that's more of a dinner dress, Mama. It's nothing to wear to the Winter Carnival Ball."

"I don't know about that one, though," her mother said slowly, shaking her head.

"I'll just try it on, all right? Then if you still

say no, we'll forget it." Gina gestured to a little gilt bench in the center of the area. "Why don't you sit there while I put it on?" Before her mother could refuse, Gina slipped into the dressing room.

When Gina finally had donned the dress, she looked into the mirror, and a little gasp of pleasure escaped her lips. The burgundy brightened her warm olive skin. The heart-shaped neckline softened the lines of her face, and the high, puffed sleeves cast a delicate glow on her face and made her eyes glitter like black gems. The long lines of the snug midriff made her look taller and slimmer. She imagined herself standing side by side with Dex, posing for photographs. When Gina's glance fell to the bottom of the bell-shaped skirt, about an inch below her knees, she snickered. Black and red plaid kneesocks didn't exactly finish off the elegant look!

She was barefoot when she padded out into the store area again. *Mama just has to say yes,* she thought nervously, holding her damp palms away from the fragile fabric.

Her hopes soared when her mother took one look at her and jumped to her feet. "You look beautiful, Gina!" Mrs. Damone exclaimed. But Gina's hopes plummeted as her mother added, "But for a high school formal? Too sophisticated, I think."

A saleswoman around Mrs. Damone's age approached them in a cloud of cologne. "I'm sorry I couldn't help you before this," she apologized. "It's been terribly busy today. That dress looks fantastic on you!" she enthused, coming to Gina's rescue in the nick of time.

"You don't think it's too old for a girl of seventeen?" Mrs. Damone asked.

"Oh, not at all," the woman assured her cheerfully. "That color is very big at school dances. They go in for burgundy and deep blues a lot these days. And it's quite modest actually. To tell you the truth, I've seen women in their twenties try that style on and it's too young for them. Only someone your daughter's age can wear those puffed sleeves."

"Yes, I can see that." Gina's mother still didn't sound convinced.

"Stacy Harcourt's on the Court, and she's wearing a strapless." Gina pleaded her case. "Next to her, I'll look all covered up in this. Oh, Mama, please say yes! I know I won't find anything else I like this much. I feel like it was made for me!"

Smiling, her mother nodded. "All right, if you love it that much," she agreed. As Gina let out a muffled whoop of joy, she added to the saleswoman, "Two against one. I know when I'm licked."

"You'll take this, then?"

"Yes." Mrs. Damone smiled at Gina, who impulsively hugged her mother.

Gina hurried upstairs almost as soon as she was in the front door of her house. In her room, she took the dress from her shopping bag and lovingly unfolded the cloud of velvet, shaking out every wrinkle before she spread it out on her bed. She stood for several minutes admiring her purchase.

As soon as she hung up the dress, she called Tess. "You lucky thing!" Tess exclaimed when Gina told her what she'd gotten. "It sounds scrumptious. I've been working on my dress half the day myself, and you know, it doesn't look bad at all. But have I got a headache! Did you ever try to sew on seed pearls? They're so tiny you can hardly see the hole to put the needle through. I'm going to take two aspirin and rest up for the game tonight. Otherwise, every time I cheer, it's going to split my head open!"

"Well, you don't have to pick me up tonight," Gina told her. "That should give you a few more minutes to take it easy. My folks can just drop me off at school on their way to their friends' house."

"Sure you won't change your mind about Marsha's party?"

"No, Tess, not tonight. I really can't. Besides," she added before her friend could ask any more questions, "I want to save all my energy for next week so I can dance all night."

"Me, too! Last year's Winter Carnival Ball was the best dance of the whole year. You don't know what you missed! I went with Zack Wenner and still had a great time—that should tell you how much fun it was."

"That's right. How could you ever have had such a crush on Zack, Tess?"

"What can I tell you? I thought he was such a hunk, Gina! Hulk's more like it. That guy goes through life like it's one big football field." She giggled. "Too many tackles for me. Mary Bowes is welcome to him. By the way, you're welcome to borrow any of my makeup if you need any special colors to go with your dress."

"I'll bet that champagne shadow you've got would go just great with . . ." Gina's voice faded as a sobering realization hit her. There was no way she could put her makeup on at home the night of the dance: her parents wouldn't let her leave the house if she did!

"You still there?" Tess asked.

"Uh, sure, I'm here. I, um, suddenly remembered the other reason I was calling." She forced a laugh. "We got so busy talking, I completely forgot. Do you think it would be okay if Dex picked me up at your house before the dance? My parents may be having company in and I hate to have to parade around in front of everyone. Besides, then you could help me with my makeup. You're so much better at it than I am."

"Of course it's all right," Tess assured her. "You can bring all your clothes and just get ready here. It'll be fun."

As Gina hung up, she was already searching for a believable excuse to give her folks for going to the Ball from Tess's house. Unplugging the telephone extension from her wall jack and returning it to the bedside table in her parents' room, she told herself she had a whole week to create a story for her mother and father.

As her parents and Dino prepared to go to the Genoveses' house, Gina showered and changed into her uniform. As usual, she left her face naked except for a dusting of blusher and a smidgen of lipstick. But before she left her room, she dug out her secret cache of cosmetics from her dresser drawer and tucked eye liner, shadow, and mascara into the little tote bag that held her hairspray, extra pair of tights, and the other paraphernalia that she took to every game.

"Ready, Gina?" her father shouted from the foot of the stairs. "We should get going if we're going to drop you at the school and still get to the Genoveses' on time."

"I'm on my way!" she answered, turning off the light and closing the door behind her.

"I'll pick you up right here after the game," her father told her as he dropped Gina off at the curb in front of the school. "Nine-thirty, you said?"

"Even if there's overtime, it shouldn't last more than two and a half hours," Gina told him as she got out. "And if Midvale's team is as good as it should be this year, there's no question of overtime. We'll slaughter them!"

"Good luck," her father wished her as he put the car in gear again.

The temperature had dropped with the sun, and Gina shivered in her lightweight jacket as she walked up the path to the school. Since she was early, she stopped to finish her makeup in the regular first-floor girls' room instead of going straight to the locker room. That way, she could avoid having to explain why she hadn't put on her makeup at home.

When Gina entered the locker room a few minutes later, Kathy Phillips was there, standing at the makeup mirror with an array of little plastic cases and gold-capped crayons spread out on the shallow shelf in front of her.

"Oh, hi, Gina!" She wheeled around, her eyes startled. "You're early tonight."

"Sorry if I scared you, Kath. I didn't expect anybody else to be here so soon. My folks are going out, so they dropped me off. How come you're here so early?"

"I came with Rich. The team's got to be here way ahead of time, you know." She looked down at the cosmetics scattered in front of her and shrugged. "I don't mind being the first one here, since it gives me plenty of time to get ready. I hate putting on my makeup at home. Mom's always threatening to make me march back upstairs and wash my face."

"Your mother's strict about makeup?" Gina asked, amazed.

"Oh, sure," Kathy replied casually, uncapping a pencil. "Isn't everyone's? I can't think of a single girl who doesn't put more makeup on after she gets to school. Even Tess's mother bugs her about it, and her mom's more like one of the gang than a mother."

"I thought my folks were about the only ones," Gina admitted.

"Are you serious? Sherri's mother would be happier if Sherri didn't even wear *lipstick.*" Kathy chuckled. "My mom's big line is, 'You'll have plenty of time for that when you're older, dear.' She acts like you never wear makeup until you need it!"

"My mother's the same," Gina confessed. "I even hide my eye shadows and stuff at home."

Kathy just nodded, and Gina continued on to her locker. It was weird, but she felt almost as if she'd dropped a bombshell that had turned out to be a dud. She'd wasted all that energy locking herself in a stall in the girls' room and sneaking her makeup on!

She remembered a time in Brooklyn when she was eleven. After weeks of feeling like a criminal, she'd confessed to her two best friends that at times she couldn't stand her little brother and almost wished he hadn't been born. She'd expected both Karen and Angie to gasp in shock or tell her she was horrible. Instead, they'd both admitted feeling the same way about their own brothers and sisters. Gina had felt as if a weight had been lifted from her shoulders, but she'd felt a little let down as well, just the way she felt about this latest discovery.

One by one, the other girls trickled in, and the locker room buzzed with last-minute gossip, all of which came to an instant halt when Ms. Bowen stuck her head in through the door leading to the gym and blew her whistle.

"Come on, gang, let's go!" Stacy yelled. "Ready, Gina?"

"Ready—and nervous," Gina admitted.

"Being a captain's no different from being a cheerleader," Stacy said with a matter-of-factness that calmed Gina as they headed for the door. "The only difference is you're cheering on the rest of the squad as well as the spectators. You can do it!"

EIGHT

Gina breathed deeply as she and Stacy led the rest of the girls into the gym, where the stands were filled to the rafters. She shoved her purse beneath the section of the bottom row on the home side reserved for the squad, then stood at attention for "The Star-Spangled Banner."

As soon as the last note of the national anthem died out, Stacy nudged Gina, and the two of them jogged into the center of the floor, the other four girls close on their heels.

They clapped four beats to set the rhythm, then swung right into the welcoming song, which they sang facing their rivals.

As she turned to execute a back jump toward Midvale's own spectators, Gina tingled with the joy of performing.

For the rest of the game, she was too busy

conferring with Stacy or leading cheers to remember to scan the bleachers for Dex. Hanover's team worked smoothly, never letting Midvale keep the lead for long. That meant the Mustang cheerleaders had to stay on their toes, too, switching from "Hit That Hoop" to "Take the Ball Away" at the flick of a fumble or a steal.

It was as exciting as any first game of the season could possibly be, with both the Mustangs and the Rovers playing as if they were in the running for the division championship. Both Dave Prentice and Rich Stinson executed some notable plays, much to the delight of Tess and Kathy.

The score was close, with Midvale winning by just two points. As the ref blew the final whistle, the Midvale bleachers exploded with shouting, cheering, hugging, and victory signs. "We did it!" Stacy crowed joyfully as she grabbed Gina in a bear hug.

"I'm so excited!" Gina answered, equally ecstatic. "And being cocaptain makes it even better!"

"If I had to be cocaptain with anybody, I'm glad it's with you, Gina," Stacy admitted. "You really did more than your part to keep everyone up and lively. Think how exciting it's going to be when we win the basketball championship."

"That's a long way off," Tess, who'd made it a three-way hug, reminded them.

"Don't be a spoilsport," Stacy chided, laughing from sheer exhilaration. "Just make sure Dave keeps making those incredible shots!"

"He was great, wasn't he?" Tess said happily, not waiting for an answer before she went over to throw her arms around her mother, who'd climbed down from the bleachers and was talking to the Callahans and Patricia Petersen's dad.

"Hey, look at that!" Stacy muttered. "Either Patricia's got a sister she hasn't told us about or her father really *is* robbing the cradle!"

"She doesn't look all that young," Gina said, trying not to stare at the dark-haired woman hanging onto Phil Petersen's arm. "She must be at least twenty-five."

Stacy shrugged. "To each his own, right? You and Dex going over to Marsha's?"

"I'm not. I don't know if Dex is or not. I'm just going to the dance with him, Stacy. Our first date," she pointedly reminded her cocaptain.

"Oh, I'm sure he'll be there," Stacy said airily. "It's not like Dex to miss a chance to show off."

"How come you're so hostile about him?"

Gina asked. "I thought you liked Dex. After all, you went out with him yourself, remember?"

"I did like him." Stacy shook her head. "I guess he's okay. Let's just say we didn't hit it off in a big way. I don't mean to sound like such a witch, Gina. I'm sure you'll have a great time with Dex."

"So am I," Gina said stiffly. Stacy's attitude toward Dex annoyed her. It was as if Stacy were implying a date with Dex was nothing to look forward to.

"Look, I'd better get going," Gina said. "I'm being picked up outside at nine and I've still got to get my stuff together."

"You're really not going to Marsha's?" Stacy raised her eyebrows.

"Not tonight," Gina said shortly, walking away before Stacy could ask why not.

In the locker room, she quickly washed her face, then grabbed her coat and left before the other girls tore themselves away from their families and other team supporters. She didn't want to deal with one more question about Marsha's party.

The front hall was clustered with groups of milling students and adults as Gina wriggled to the door, but Dex was nowhere to be seen. She sighed as she pushed her way through the front door and felt the first cold blast of air on her overheated face. *I wish I were going to Marsha's party instead of waiting for Dad to pick me up!* she thought. But there was only a chance Dex was going to Marsha's, and her parents never would have given her permission to go, not when there was a gathering at the Genoveses' house.

She raced down the path as soon as she saw the family station wagon approaching, so she could reach it just as it slid up to the curb and before anybody saw her leaving. It couldn't hurt to have everyone think she had somewhere more exciting to be than Marsha Steiner's party, even though nothing could be further from the truth.

"Capture! That's your fourth pair, Gina. One more and I win!"

"Don't be so smug," Gina teased Tony Genovese from the other side of the Genoveses' dining room table. Smiling triumphantly, she placed one of her green stones on the Pente board between them.

"Uh-oh," Tony muttered, seeing how she'd managed to hem in two of his yellow stones. "I didn't even see that one coming."

"Now I've got eight of your guys, too."

Deftly, Gina reached down and plucked the two captured stones from the board, adding them to the three pairs of yellow stones she'd already won. "Now we're even. One capture on either side wins."

"Hmmm. Let me think this one over."

Gina studied Tony's dark, curly hair as he leaned over the board, lost in thought. He loved to play board games as much as she did. Tess and Stacy would probably think she was crazy if she told them she loved to play Pente. She couldn't imagine spending an evening with Dex this way. Of course, she didn't think she'd want to spend an evening with Dex playing Pente.

"Hah!" Tony exclaimed, depositing one of his stones on the board with a flourish. "That makes three of mine in a row in two directions. Let's see you wiggle out of that one, Damone!" He looked up, his dark eyes crinkling in amusement, his lips curved in a challenging smile.

But Gina was ready for him. "If you say so," she said demurely, unhesitatingly reaching for one of her unplayed stones and setting it on a spot she'd been hoping he'd overlook. "Five green in a row. That's the game."

"I don't believe it!" Tony stared at the grid between them. "That's five in a row all right. You know, I didn't even see those four. Too busy plotting my killer moves, I guess." He laughed. "That makes two games for you, two for me. Want to play one more, as a tie breaker?"

"Sure, why not?" Gina retrieved all her green stones, pushing the eight of Tony's she'd captured back to his side of the table. "Loser starts."

"That's right. Rub it in," he chided.

The Genoveses' big old house on the outskirts of Chicago was warm and cozy, the air perfumed with the scent of rich espresso and sweet anisette cookies. Where Gina and Tony sat was an island of quiet calm between two noisy oceans. From the kitchen came the high-pitched voices of Dino, the DiPietro girls, and Tony's little sister, Maria, involved in an argumentative game of Junior Trivial Pursuit. In the living room, the adults—Gina's own parents, the Genoveses, the DiPietros, and old Mr. and Mrs. Gagliano—conversed in Italian so rapid-fire it was almost incomprehensible to Gina, whose own Italian was rusty from lack of use.

"What are they talking about in there, anyway?" she asked Tony after he'd put a yellow stone in the center of the board. Even though Tony had been born in Illinois, he spoke Italian more fluently than she did.

He chuckled as she made her move. "Bread."

"Bread?"

He nodded as he set his second stone on the board. "Mrs. DiPietro says the bread at Giovanni's Bakery is the best Italian bread in all of the Chicago area, and your mom's insisting you can't get decent bread here because the water's different from the water in Sicily. You need the right water for the proper bread, she says."

"Really!" Gina sighed. "Seven years in this country, and you'd think my folks had just gotten off the boat. Your move, Tony."

"They can't help the way they are," Tony said gently. "I guess it's not easy for people like our folks and the Gaglianos and the twins' parents, being brought up the old way like they were. Look at my mom and dad—they've been American citizens a lot longer than yours, and my mom still goes on about how impersonal the American supermarkets are compared to the friendly neighborhood shops back in Palermo. And she knows better, too. When we were in Italy three years ago, there weren't nearly as many little shops as there used to be. There were supermarkets all over the place."

"Isn't it awful, though?" Gina asked, looking up from the board. It was her move, but she was more interested in talking than playing. "It's like not being a real American."

"Do you really think so?" Tony looked surprised. "I don't feel that way at all. The way I see it, we have the best of both worlds—all the benefits of America along with the culture and heritage of an ancient civilization. I like that a lot."

"You really do, don't you?" It was different for Tony, of course. He was a boy, so his parents weren't as strict as hers. For him, being Italian didn't mean having twice as many rules as everyone else or not being able to stay out late or feeling different from all the other kids at his school.

He beat her in four more moves. "I give up," she cheerfully conceded. "Three out of five. You're the champion!"

"Wait'll next week," Tony promised, his eyes sparkling. "You and I can match wits with Trivial Pursuit. I'll probably beat you at that, too!"

"You're going to have to wait," she told him. "I won't be going to the DiPietros' next week."

"You won't? How come?" A shadow of disappointment crossed his attractive features.

"It's the night of Midvale's big Winter Carnival Ball," Gina explained. "Much as I'd like to play Trivial Pursuit with you, I think I'd rather dance."

"Oh?" Tony swiveled in his seat to put the boxed game back inside the dining room sideboard. "Got a date?"

"Do I ever! Just one of the neatest guys in the whole school," she said proudly.

"I guess a girl like you can have her pick of dates, huh? Pretty, popular, and a cheerleader."

"No way," she insisted, but she felt her cheeks flush with pleasure. "I'm just satisfied that this particular one finally asked me out. Don't you have a winter ball of some sort at your school?"

Tony shook his head. "We used to, but this year the senior class council decided to spend twice as much money on the prom. We're having it at the Lake Club in Evanston instead of in the school gym. That means we can't afford a winter dance, too."

"Neat! What a great idea! I guess you're a big deal now, being a class officer and everything."

"No way." He grinned as he repeated the phrase she'd used earlier. "I'm vice president of the senior class, but the position doesn't have a whole lot of power connected to it. All four of us—the president, secretary, treasurer, and me—decide what we'd like to do, and then the whole class gets to vote on anything important. Mostly the officers get a lot of the drudge work, heading decoration committees and all that. All work and no play," he insisted, putting on an exaggerated look of self-pity. "It's not a glamour job like being a cheerleader."

"Glamour job my foot!" Gina sputtered. But she was laughing when she added, "I sure didn't feel glamorous tonight. I was terrified we might lose the game! I feel so responsible, being on the cheering squad. As if it's up to me to make the players want to succeed."

"You still have practices all the time?" Tony asked curiously.

"At least two days a week after school, sometimes three," Gina answered. "And we have a pep rally on Fridays if there's a game over the weekend."

"I guess that doesn't leave you a lot of spare time."

"Oh, it's not really that bad," Gina said. "Even when there's practice, I'm home before Mom gets in from work."

"Maybe after I get my car next week—" Tony began.

"You're getting a car? Tony, that's great!" Gina exclaimed. "What I wouldn't give for a car of my own. Do you have one picked out already?"

He nodded. "I've made the down payment and everything. I'm just waiting for the loan to go through, which shouldn't be a problem since Dad cosigned for me. Wait till you see these wheels!" His voice quickened with pleasure. "A fire engine red Firebird!"

"Simple and unpretentious, huh?" Gina asked innocently.

"You got it!" Tony laughed. "Just like me. Anyhow, what I was going to say is—"

He didn't get a chance to say anything, because Mrs. Damone chose that moment to pop up in the doorway between the dining and living rooms. "Time to go, Gina. You too, Dino," she added in a louder voice.

"Okay, Mom," Dino called back. "I just have to answer this one question and I've won the game."

"I'm glad somebody in our family's not disgracing the Damone name," Gina said ruefully. "You should have seen Tony, Mom. He massacred me at Pente!"

"Not quite," he contradicted her. "I'm just at my best under pressure."

A loud victory cry from the kitchen assured them all that Dino had won. "Nobody's ever going to accuse you and Dino of letting the girls win," Gina kidded as she got to her feet. To her mother she added, "I guess we're ready."

"Come say good night to everyone and get your coat. Dino, you too!"

"Here I am." Dino stifled a yawn as he turned the corner from the kitchen, his huge brown eyes looking heavy with tiredness.

"You never finished what you were starting to say," Gina remarked to Tony as all four of them left the dining room.

"Oh, nothing important." Tony shook his head and looked from Gina to her mother to Dino. "Sorry you can't make it next week."

"We'll play Trivial Pursuit some other time," she assured him, but he'd already turned away and was kidding around with his little sister, who'd followed them in.

As she settled into her seat, Gina caught herself fighting off sleep. "I'm pretty beat my-self," she commented, yawning as Mr. Damone merged into traffic on the expressway to Midvale.

"You had a busy night, didn't you?" Her mother turned around in the front seat. "Look at your brother, would you? Asleep already! He always has such a good time with the Gen-oveses."

"I had a good time, too," Gina admitted sleepily, remembering her low expectations as she was leaving the school building. "Tony's a lot of fun."

"He's a nice boy, isn't he?" her mother said warmly. "Was he disappointed that you won't be going with him to your Ball next week?"

"Disappointed?" Gina shook her head. "No. Why would he be? I'm sure Tony couldn't care less about going to some dance at Midvale. I mean, he's got his own school dances."

As her mother turned back to face front and started talking softly to Mr. Damone, Gina fought to keep her eyelids open. They had developed a will of their own and wanted to close. After a moment, she gave in and shut her eyes.

When she opened them again they were parked in front of their own house, and her father was just removing the key from the ignition.

"Maybe you should carry Dino inside, Elio," her mother was saying. "It seems a shame to wake him just to make him go to bed again."

Gina followed her father, who had Dino in his arms, up the stairs to the second floor, not even stopping to hang up her jacket in the hall closet. She mumbled good night to her mother as she headed for her bedroom. In her room, Gina changed quickly into flannel pajamas, draping her jacket and uniform as neatly as possible over the old corduroy armchair in the corner next to her bed. She snuggled under the covers, half asleep even as her head hit the pillow.

NINE

Gina awoke the next morning with a plan for convincing her parents to let Dex pick her up at Tess's house the night of the dance.

Before dressing, Gina took a long, hot shower, letting the steam work on her aching muscles. Pulling on her jeans and a sweatshirt, she shoved her feet into her woolly sheepskin bedroom slippers. Before she left the room, she grabbed her jacket from the chair.

It's awfully quiet downstairs for a Sunday morning, Gina realized as she hung her jacket in the closet. Usually, she was greeted by the soundtrack of the cartoons and the sight of Dino watching them cross-legged on the living room floor, but the living room was empty.

Her mother, dressed up for church, was seated at the kitchen table with a cup of coffee and the Sunday *Tribune*.

"Morning, Mama," Gina greeted her, heading straight for the refrigerator. "Dino and Dad sleeping in?"

"No, Gina," she said, smiling. "Haven't you looked at the clock?"

The face of the clock on the kitchen wall floored her. "Twelve-fifteen! Is that thing working?"

Mrs. Damone nodded. "I guess you were even more tired than you knew. Your papa and Dino drove out to the mall after church." She made a little tsk-tsk noise, pursing her lips. "Those computer game machines! And your father is just as bad as your brother. He says it's the electronic circuits which fascinate him, but I know better. He likes to play those silly games!"

"Boys will be boys, I guess," Gina said lightly. "I read in some magazine that the reason so many men become pilots and engineers and architects is that they never stop wanting to play with toys. The toys just get bigger and more complicated."

Her mother nodded. "That may be true."

"Any hot bargains at the Jewel?"

"I was just making up my shopping list while the house was quiet. One of the markets is having a sale on California strawberries, so maybe I'll bake a strawberry ricotta cheesecake to take along to the DiPietros' house next weekend."

That gave Gina just the opening she needed. "You know, Mama, I was thinking," she began. "I know you wouldn't want my date coming to pick me up when you and Dad weren't in the house, and it doesn't seem fair if you'd have to leave the party just to come back here and meet him. . . ."

Her mother nodded. "I hadn't thought of that," she admitted, her forehead wrinkling in worry. "The DiPietros will expect us at six."

"And the dance doesn't start until eight. So I was thinking, I'm sure Tess's mom wouldn't mind if I got ready and had Dex pick me up over there."

"At Tess's house? That might be a good idea." Her mother's face brightened, but only momentarily. "But are you sure Mrs. Belding will be at home that night?"

"Pretty sure. Why don't I call right now and find out?" Gina crossed to the wall phone and started dialing Tess's number before her mother could suggest they wait until Mr. Damone got home. She hoped Tess's mother was planning to stay in the night of the dance.

Tess answered the phone with a drowsy, "Hello?"

"Hi, it's Gina. How was the party?"

Tess awoke instantly. "A real doozy! I didn't get home until close to two, and I ate enough to feed an army. Lots of people asked where you were, Gina. Dex didn't stay very long—I think he was hoping you'd show up."

"Really?" Gina asked, feeling a twinge of pleasure and surprise. "Well, he did say he had another party to go to."

"I'll bet he'd have stayed at Marsha's if you'd been there, though. How was your night?"

"Oh, it was nice," Gina said simply. "Listen," she went on, "the reason I'm calling is, my mom says it's all right for me to be picked up at your place next week as long as your mother's going to be there. Is she?"

"She'll be here," Tess answered, sounding a bit grim. "She's busy cleaning out the basement and packing stuff up already so she can put the house on the market as soon as the divorce is final. Want me to get her so she can talk to your mother herself?"

"That might be good. Here, Mama." Gina turned toward her mother, holding out the receiver. "Tess is getting Mrs. Belding so she can talk to you."

Trying to maintain her nonchalance, Gina

crossed to the counter and poured herself a bowl of cornflakes. But she listened hard to every word that came out of her mother's mouth, not relaxing until Mrs. Damone said, "All right, then. We'll drop Gina off at your house at five-thirty. I really appreciate your being so helpful."

Me, too, Gina thought emphatically.

"And good luck with selling your house," her mother finished before saying good bye.

"What a shame Tess and her mother have to move." Mrs. Damone was shaking her head solemnly when Gina returned to the table with her cornflakes. "It must be terrible, getting a divorce and having to start all over that way."

"It can't be much fun," Gina agreed, but her mind wasn't on the Beldings' divorce. "Is everything all set then?"

"All set? Oh, for you to go to the Beldings' house on Saturday? Yes, dear, she said she's happy to have you. Your papa and I will just have to wait to meet your date when he brings you home."

"Oh, I know you'll like him," Gina said happily, spooning up a heap of cereal. Now that the knot in her stomach had untied itself, she was ravenous. She ate hungrily, satisfied that nothing could go wrong.

* * *

The following Monday, Gina was a little disappointed to find that Dex treated her exactly as he always had. He was friendly, and he joked and flirted with her in history class, but he was casual and not especially attentive.

On Tuesday it was announced that Friday's game with Colebrook High would be canceled because of a flu epidemic there. "We're going to have our work cut out for us for the next two weeks, girls," Ms. Bowen told the squad at that afternoon's practice. "By next week, everybody's still going to be worrying about the epidemic spreading to Midvale. And we'll have more on our hands than that."

"You mean Midvale fans are going to lose momentum?" Gina asked.

"Right. Without a game to keep them going, team supporters tend to lose interest and enthusiasm. So you six are going to have your hands full."

"Maybe we should start practicing that double splits routine instead of saving it for the semifinals," Gina suggested, adding, after a muffled groan from Tess, "Stacy and I can work extra with anybody who has trouble with it." She hated forcing poor Tess to do a routine that intimidated her, but as cocaptain Gina knew her responsibility was to the whole school and not any particular girl. "What do you think, Stacy?"

"I think it's a pretty good idea," Stacy agreed. "But with the dance and all coming up, maybe it's the wrong time to start on something new."

"Do you think it could be modified, Gina?" Ms. Bowen asked. "Maybe you could leave out some steps, make it simpler? Without making it look any less spectacular, of course."

Gina nodded. "I should be able to. Why don't we just work on the basic double splits today?" she suggested. "Then I can map out a new routine at home tonight, go over it with Stacy tomorrow, and have it ready for Thursday's practice. Are we going to be having an extra practice Friday since there's no pep rally?"

"That's fine with me, but maybe the squad should vote on it," Ms. Bowen said. "Want to give me a show of hands on who's willing to have extra practice Friday afternoon for as long as it takes to get through this routine?"

Gina watched apprehensively. Three other squad members would have to raise their hands if her suggestion was to be accepted. If that didn't happen, she might lose her first major challenge as cocaptain.

Sherri's hand went up immediately, which was to be expected. Nothing fazed Sherri. The other two juniors, Stacy, and Tess looked lost in concentration, as if they were all weighing the idea of having to practice extra hard. Gina was disappointed in Stacy for not agreeing immediately.

After what seemed like hours, Stacy stuck her hand in the air. Slowly, Kathy and Patricia followed. Raising her shoulders almost to ear level in a broad shrug, Tess grinned. Then she, too, held her hand aloft.

"Good! That's the kind of team spirit we need!" Ms. Bowen commended them. "Okay, Gina, why don't you demonstrate the moves for everyone?"

The splits, executed in a down-up-turn-down-up sequence, were the only really difficult part of the routine, though for Gina they were child's play. She performed them slowly, cautioning, "I did them too fast when I first came up with the routine and pulled a muscle in my thigh, so remember to take it gradually." The only other new moves were some double kicks. "You can start practicing these on your own right away," Gina said. "Nobody should have any trouble with them."

"Maybe we should try those right after

warming up," Stacy put in, "to sort of get our legs flexed for the splits."

Gina nodded, and Stacy crossed from the bleachers where she'd been standing. "Okay, I'll be the guinea pig," she joked.

Every girl did better on the splits than Gina had expected. But there was definitely room for improvement. "Help me, I'm stuck!" Patricia screeched once, stuck in mid-split, before she toppled over. Tess had just the opposite problem when she slid down for the first split, then couldn't raise herself back up again.

"Now what?" she asked indignantly as she tried to push her uncooperative body off the ground. "Do you all run up and carry me off the floor and out of the gym like this?" But she didn't give up. After bending her knees and struggling to a sideways crouching position, she got to her feet again and managed to get through the second split without failure.

"When I did the routine in competition, I did those double splits twice, remember?" Gina asked as practice drew to a close. "I think we can save them and do them only once—at the very end. That should make it a lot easier for everyone."

"You're not kidding! That way, if I flub it again, I'll only have to be carried off at the end and everybody might think it was *supposed* to happen!" Tess quipped.

"Do you really mind having to do those splits now instead of during semifinals?" Gina asked Tess when they were heading for Nicola's.

"To tell you the truth, I did when you first suggested it," Tess admitted. "I wondered how any friend of mine could want to torture me like that." She laughed. "But after doing them, I think it's going to be all right. I'm pretty proud of myself for being able to do them at all."

"You didn't look bad," Gina assured her. "And I'm glad you're not mad at me."

"I guess you really didn't have much choice. If Ms. Bowen's right, the kids are really going to need some stirring up at next week's pep rally. We should knock 'em off their feet with this one!"

When they arrived at Nicola's, Gina learned that the others were as enthusiastic as Tess. She worked hard that night to pare down the movements without making the routine too simple, and by practice Thursday she was satisfied all the girls would have mastered the choreography in plenty of time.

By Friday, Gina was checking the time hourly. Friday evening seemed interminable. Gina watched a TV movie with her parents at eight o'clock, and she went to bed immediately afterward just to make the time pass more quickly. As the week's tension drained from her body, Gina was quickly drowsy. The last thing she thought before she dozed off was that when she opened her eyes again, the day she'd been waiting for finally would have arrived.

TEN

"Gina, you look incredible! That dress is too much. I swear it looks as if someone made it just for you!"

"You really think so?" Gina asked Tess, turning away from the full-length mirror on the back of Tess's bedroom door.

"That's not a real question, is it?" Tess asked brightly. "I mean, you've got to know how fabulous you look!"

"Thanks to you. I could never have gotten my makeup to look so professional," Gina admitted, turning once again to admire herself. "You should find out about becoming one of those people who do makeovers at the cosmetics counters in Haynes's! You're better than the people who get paid for it. And thanks again for lending me these earrings." She raised a hand to one of the imitation amethysts dangling from her earlobes. "I didn't think about how dull my gold studs were going to look."

She turned to face her friend again. "Come on, now it's your turn. Let's see how your brand-new dress looks!"

"You'd never know it was the same old thing, would you?" Tess asked happily, sliding the lilac cloud of fabric from its hanger. "I'm really thrilled with how nicely it turned out."

"You should be," Gina assured her, helping Tess slip the dress over her head. "Those pearls really did the trick."

"Wait. You haven't seen the best part!" Tess insisted, shaking out a length of gathered tulle and satin she picked up from one of the twin beds in the room. As Tess fastened it around her waist, Gina saw it was a sheer overskirt of a slightly deeper lilac with a yoked satin waistband to match the dress itself.

"You look super," Gina told Tess as she perched on the edge of the twin bed closest to the vanity, careful not to crush the burgundy velvet. "And those earrings are the best! Where did you ever find any that matched the seed pearls?"

"That was just dumb luck," Tess admitted,

fluffing up her hair with a pick for the fourth time since she'd washed it. "I'd just found these little lavender seed pearls at the fabric shop—you know that place at the end of the mall?—and I thought I'd duck into the Brigitte Shop for a second."

"The Brigitte Shop?" Gina raised her eyebrows. "I thought that place was far out of our price range for sure."

"Oh, it is, but— Well, to be honest, I was dying to find out how much Stacy had paid for her dress. I didn't see another dress like hers anywhere in the shop and I was getting all sort of antsy. Places like that, the salesgirls follow you around like you're a shoplifter and they're just waiting to catch you red-handed! I'd just decided to get out of there before somebody came up and told me I didn't belong there when I passed the jewelry counter and saw these earrings *and* a big sale sign. So now Stacy's not the only one with something from Brigitte's!" She laughed. "And the best part is, they were just eight dollars, marked all the way down from twenty!"

Gina glanced at her wrist, forgetting she'd tucked her sporty wristwatch into her gold clutch bag. "Darn! By the time I get used to not wearing a watch, I'll be putting it back on again. Do you know what time it is?"

"Look behind you. There's a little alarm clock on the bedside table."

"Just a few minutes past seven!" Gina inhaled deeply in frustration. "I just knew we'd be ready too early!"

"Would you stop fidgeting? You're even making *me* nervous!" Tess scolded her, smiling.

"I'm sorry—I just can't help it. I've been on pins and needles all day," Gina admitted.

"Let's go wait in the living room." Tess pushed back the bench and got to her feet. "Maybe having my mom make a fuss over you will calm you down."

Gina jumped up readily, grabbing the big shopping bag that held her jeans and sweater and the makeup she'd brought over. The quilted black velvet coat her mother was letting her borrow for the Ball was hanging in the Beldings' front closet.

Mrs. Belding was sitting on the cushioned chintz couch in the living room, looking like a teenager in her faded jeans and untucked red flannel shirt. She was so intent on the clipboard balanced on one knee she didn't hear the girls enter.

"What's that, Mom?" Tess asked, causing her mother to look up with startled eyes.

"Oh, hi, girls! I was just trying to make a list of what gets packed, what can be sold, and what goes to Goodwill when we move. It's mind-boggling how much junk gets acquired in twenty years. But don't you two look striking!" She flung the clipboard aside.

"What do you think of Gina's makeup, Mom? I did it for her."

"*Very* good, Tess. I should let you experiment on me one of these days before I've let myself go totally to pot."

"Sure thing, Mom. But you have to let me do your hair, too. Is it okay if Gina and I split a Coke?"

Mrs. Belding jumped to her feet. "Let me get it for you, hon. You're likely to splash something all over your dress if you do it. How about Tess's dress, Gina?" she asked, her face now glowing with pride. "Didn't she outdo herself this time?"

"It's beautiful, isn't it?" Gina agreed, carefully settling herself on the end of the couch while Tess flopped down as usual on the reclining chair next to the sofa.

Tess was shaking her head as her mother

left the room. "I wish Mom wouldn't mope around like this."

"At least she's not bursting her seams," Gina said. "Patricia told me her mom gained thirty pounds in just a month after the Petersens separated."

"She can thank me for that," Tess said, keeping her voice low. "Mom knows I've just got to *look* at a potato chip or a pretzel to blow up like a blimp. She's never allowed junk food in the house, so she can't start now." Tess scowled. "Gina! Stop that! I know darned well you're trying to sneak a peek at your watch. When Dex gets here, he gets here. He'll probably beat Dave in that Porsche of his."

"Just what makes you think I was trying to see the time?" Gina asked indignantly as she whipped a tissue out of her bag. She pretended to blow her nose, but she should have known better than to try to fool Tess. As soon as she put the tissue back in her purse and looked at her friend, they both giggled.

"Here you go, girls." Mrs. Belding came back into the room, a soft drink in each hand.

"Thank you, Mrs. Belding," Gina said, reaching for hers, then almost dropping it as the front doorbell rang. Tightening her grip, she brought the glass to her lips and swallowed. For an instant, as Mrs. Belding went to answer the door, she found herself wishing she were going to the dance with Tony or even Arnold—anybody but Dex. At least then she wouldn't be jumping out of her skin this way, like a cat in a thunderstorm.

"Sit back and smile, for goodness' sake!" Tess hissed. "You look like you're about to go to the electric chair."

Gina took a deep breath, then reached for her glass again. Without something to hold on to, her arms didn't feel right no matter how casually she tried to keep them at her sides or fold them in her lap.

"Here's Dex, Gina!" Mrs. Belding announced brightly, coming back from the hall with Dex following close on her heels.

"Hey, Gina. Hey, Tess," Dex greeted them, holding his right hand like a cocked gun and pointing it first at one and then the other.

"Hi, Dex," Gina heard herself saying in a voice that sounded exactly like her normal one, and not as weak as she felt.

"Hey, handsome," Tess said lightly.

Truer words were never spoken, Gina thought, not listening as Tess started complaining about Dave being late. Dex looked better than ever, not at all like a high school kid in his tux and white pleated shirt. He wore a narrow satin bow tie in almost the same shade of burgundy as Gina's dress.

"Hey, look, you two match!" Tess interrupted herself delightedly.

"So that's why you asked what color dress I'd be wearing!"

Dex grinned, looking pleased with himself. "For this, too," he said, bringing his left hand up so Gina could see it held a corsage box.

"Oooh, let me see!" Gina sprang to her feet, so eager to find out what her flowers looked like that she didn't even feel nervous.

She opened the box and gasped in pleasure. "They're beautiful! Look, Tess," she said, holding the box so her friend could see the delicate blossoms of white, russet, and gold held together with a lacy gold bow. "I've never seen anything like these before."

"They're orchids," Dex said simply. "Want me to pin them on for you?"

"Orchids? I thought they only came in

purple and were gigantic," Tess said. "Like all the grandmas wear on Mother's Day."

"Those are just one type of orchid, dear," Mrs. Belding told her. Turning to Gina, she added, "They'll look perfect with your dress."

Gina started to hand Dex the box, then changed her mind. "Maybe I shouldn't put them on till we get to the school," she said. "I'd hate to crush them with my coat."

"Whatever you want." Dex shrugged.

"I'll get my coat." Gina put the lid back on the box and gave it to Dex as she passed him on the way to the hall.

"Can I stick this in the trunk of your car?" She was holding her shopping bag as she reentered the living room.

"Isn't this dance just for one night?" Dex asked suavely.

Gina glared at Tess, who'd allowed a snort of laughter to escape her lips. "It's just the clothes I wore over here this afternoon," she explained. "Thanks again for letting me come over, Mrs. Belding."

"Of course, Gina. Any time."

"Are you guys really going off and leaving me here? What if Dave stands me up?"

"Were you supposed to be going to the dance with Dave Prentice?" Dex asked Tess in mock puzzlement. "That's funny, 'cause I passed him on the way over here. He had a gorgeous blond on his arm."

Now it was Gina's turn to chuckle at Tess, who glared at Dex. "Cute, Grantham, real cute."

"We'll see you there," Gina told her as they left.

Dave passed them on the front walk. "I'm not real late, am I?" he asked. "Stupid car takes a year to warm up in this weather."

"You're early, Prentice," Dex told him. "Tess was just getting in the shower as we were leaving."

"You're terrible!" Gina laughed as Dave stopped dead in his tracks before hurrying on toward the house.

"Not really," he said innocently as he opened the car door for her. "When you get to know me, I'm a real prince."

She sighed as she leaned back against the luxurious leather seats. Then, remembering her one experience with Dex's driving habits, she reached over and fastened her seatbelt. She wanted to step out of this silver chariot looking like Cinderella, not like one of the ugly stepsisters with her hair flying in all directions and her dress mussed up from being hurled all over the front seat.

Sometimes, she told herself with a smile as Dex got in and started the engine, *even a princess has to be a little bit practical!*

ELEVEN

The Midvale High School gymnasium had never looked better than it did the night of the Winter Carnival Ball. "If you didn't look down at the floor, you'd never even know it was a gym," Dave Prentice observed when he and Tess arrived.

"The gym does look spectacular," Gina agreed, looking around the table where the four of them sat with Todd Solomon, Sherri, Sherri's brother Dennis, and Janet Perry.

"I get some credit for that," Janet chimed in. "I was on the decorating committee."

"What about me?" Dennis looked injured. "Don't I get some credit for making all that snow for you?"

"Snow by Dennis Callahan, gang!" Janet grinned.

The snow was white confetti scattered all

over the floor so it almost hid the regular gym markings. The bleachers had been folded and the walls draped in crepe paper—white representing snow-covered landscapes and royal blue for the winter sky. From the rafters hung icicles of clear cellophane along with intricate construction-paper snowflakes.

A small raised platform had been erected in one corner at the far end of the room to serve as a bandstand for Lake Shore Drive, a local band that played top-40 songs mixed with the old standards that were always trotted out for high school dances. Also at that end of the room stood the queen's throne, flanked on either side by six smaller chairs for her attendants. Close inspection revealed that the throne was simply a wicker peacock chair draped in white satin held in place by pale blue satin ribbons and white artificial roses. The attendants' seats were folding chairs similarly draped in ice-blue satin with white ribbons.

As the band swung into a romantically slow version of "Time After Time," Dex reached over and took Gina's hand. "Let's go, Gina. Here I'm with the best dancer in the school, and we haven't been on the floor yet tonight."

"I've always loved this song," Gina murmured dreamily, closing her eyes as her body melted into Dex's and followed his lead. Gina was aware of nothing but the romantic strains of the ballad and the gentle pressure of Dex's arm around her waist and his hand lightly cradling hers against his chest.

"Hey, you really are good," Dex said, his voice low and husky, as they continued dancing right into the next slow number. "We should have done this before."

"You should have asked me," Gina teased, her confidence growing as the evening passed.

When they returned to the table following a third, faster dance, a drum roll from the band signaled the time for the crowning of the queen. Dex leaned close to Gina and murmured in her ear, "I know everybody says Stacy's going to be queen, but I think you'd look better on that throne."

"Thanks for the compliment," Gina said dryly, "but Stacy's going to make a perfect queen. In that blue dress and with her blond hair—I mean, she's just the type, isn't she?"

Dex raised an eyebrow. "You think so? Maybe she's got the typical look for it, but so what? Who needs a Winter Carnival Queen who's stuck up and goes around letting everyone know she thinks she deserves to win? Look at her sitting over there, flipping her hair all over the place just to make sure everybody's watching!"

"Come on, Stacy's not that bad, Dex!" Gina argued, but she had to force herself not to smile at the affected way Dex jerked his chin from side to side, mimicking Stacy perfectly. "Look at all the other girls on the Court. We're all sitting up straighter now that we know our names are going to be called."

"Maybe. But Stacy's always showing off. Not like you, Gina. You don't have to make a big show just to make sure everybody notices you. They'd notice you anyplace."

"Well, you know," she said lightly, "when a girl's five four, she really stands out in a crowd!" Though her tone was bantering and her smile was casual, Gina felt anything but cool. She was glad to see a spotlight suddenly illuminate the area in front of the throne and Mrs. Foreman, the vice principal, step into its golden circle.

But Dex was determined to have the last word. As Mrs. Foreman cleared her throat and reached for the microphone, Dex said, his voice little more than a whisper, "That's why I stopped seeing Stacy, you know. She's just so selfish. Always has to have her own way."

He was silent as Mrs. Foreman began talking about the tradition of the Winter Carnival at

Midvale and the honor attached to being on the Court. But Gina still found it difficult to concentrate on what was being said. So Dex *had* been the one to ditch Stacy! She'd suspected as much, since it would explain Stacy's attitude whenever Dex was mentioned.

Two by two, Mrs. Foreman began to reel off the names of the Court attendants and their escorts as the band played "The Way You Look Tonight." Patricia and Brent were called first. As the two stepped into the spotlight, Mrs. Foreman handed Patricia a bouquet of pink and white carnations gathered in a big pink bow. Then Brent led his petite date to the chair on the right side of the throne indicated by Mrs. Foreman.

Sherri and Todd came next, Sherri looking as graceful and natural as usual, and they took their places to the left of the throne.

When Tess's name was called, she jumped to her feet and practically tugged Dave along with her to the charmed circle in the front. Gina smiled fondly as she watched.

When Mrs. Foreman announced, "Gina Damone and Dex Grantham," Gina tingled. There was something special about hearing their names linked by someone else's words.

She stood up on legs that felt strangely

liquid and was glad when she felt Dex's palm rest lightly between her shoulder blades, supporting her as they crossed the room.

As Gina accepted her flowers from Mrs. Foreman, she quickly ducked her head and buried her face in them as if to enjoy their scent. She couldn't let anyone see the tears that had suddenly welled up in her eyes. People might assume she was crying because she hadn't been named queen. She couldn't expect anybody else to share or understand her sheer happiness at this moment. Standing in the limelight with Dex Grantham by her side and a bouquet of flowers in her hand made Gina feel more a part of Midvale High than she had ever felt before. For once, she didn't suffer the slightest twinge of doubt. She belonged.

Gina sank onto her chair, tucking one ankle behind the other in front of her to disguise the trembling of her knees. Still blinking back tears, she glanced at Sherri Callahan, who returned an ecstatic wink and a smile. Sherri's smile made Gina aware that she'd been smiling, too, ever since her name had been called. Smiling more broadly, she closed her eyes, savoring the light touch of Dex's hand.

When she opened her eyes again, Valerie Masters was smiling in her carefully controlled way as she accepted her flowers from Mrs. Foreman. Next to her, Cal Lockhart, the college freshman Val had been seeing, grinned broadly in approval, making no attempt to follow Val's cool lead. *A down-to-earth boyfriend is probably just what Valerie needs,* Gina decided.

The drummer executed another thundering roll as Mrs. Foreman said gaily, "And the Midvale Winter Carnival Queen is . . ." At the tables off to the sides, Gina could see some people rolling their eyes at Mrs. Foreman's hopeless attempt at suspense. Still, Gina relished every second of the pomp surrounding the ceremony, and she silently thanked Mrs. Foreman for prolonging it.

"Stacy Harcourt!" Mrs. Foreman chirped as if astonished and thrilled. "And she's being escorted to the throne by Jeremy Edwards."

No matter what Dex had said, Stacy did make a beautiful queen. She shimmered in the spotlight as Mrs. Foreman handed her a bouquet of long-stemmed white roses swathed in ice-blue satin.

As soon as Stacy was seated and Jeremy had settled the queen's glittering rhinestone crown atop her head, the spectators began cheering and the photographers moved in, popping their flashbulbs for the local paper as well as the school's own *Sentinel*.

When the photographers were finished, the escorts led the Court onto the dance floor. As Gina nestled her head against Dex's warm chest, she knew she wouldn't need pictures to remember this evening. The Winter Carnival Ball would live in her memories forever.

TWELVE

"Home? Who said anything about going home?" Dex asked, looking at Gina as if she had suggested they rob the First National Bank of Chicago.

The Ball had just ended, and Dex and Gina stood facing each other in the school parking lot.

"Well, I thought—" Gina began.

"All I said was did you mind if we didn't go to Nicola's with the rest of the mob. That place is one big bore as far as I'm concerned. But I didn't say anything about going home. It's early." To illustrate this point, he held up his watch so she could see its face illuminated by the overhead security lamps.

"Eleven-thirty," she said aloud.

"Yeah, early. That's what I said." He began walking in the direction of the car again. "Come on, Gina, we'll find something better to do than sit around Nicola's listening to the same old people saying the same old things."

Gina walked silently with no idea what to do. She should have told Dex earlier that her parents expected her to be home by midnight. Now it would mean looking childish.

"What do you say to a little cruising?" Dex asked. "We can just drive around a little."

"Okay," she agreed. "But I shouldn't get home too late." She faked a yawn even though she felt wide awake. "The dance really did me in. Besides," she added, making a feeble attempt at honesty, "I didn't see my folks to tell them when I'd be home, so they'll probably be waiting up."

He gave her another suspicious look. "Your folks can't expect you home by midnight the night of a big dance, can they?" He laughed. "What are you, Cinderella or something?"

Gina smiled thinly. She *had* felt so much like Cinderella just a little while before. But at the time, she hadn't considered that she shared a curfew with the fairy-tale princess. From the way Dex spoke, she knew she must have been the only girl at the Ball whose parents expected her to come right home afterward. She and Dex had been getting along too well all evening to ruin everything because of a curfew. "Oh, I don't have to be home," she said lightly. "I'd just hate for them to be worrying."

He shrugged. "We'll take a drive, then I'll drop you off, okay? I can always go to Nicola's by myself if I feel like staying out."

"I've got to be in good shape next week," Gina said casually, trying not to sound as if she were manufacturing an explanation. "Ms. Bowen's worried that the kids won't be psyched up for the game next week, since this week's game was canceled."

"When's next week's game?" Dex asked, taking the turn that led to the highway and Brinton's Lake.

"Saturday. But we've got a pep rally Friday at school, during last period."

"Want to go to the movies Friday night? There's a couple of good flicks starting at the mall that day I'd like to catch," Dex asked offhandedly.

Gina's pulse raced, but she kept her voice as neutral and noncommittal as his had been. "Sure, that sounds like fun."

"It's a date, then," he said, smiling at her now. "Hey, look, it's starting to snow! They picked the right night for the Winter Carnival Ball, didn't they?"

"If they'd waited, we could have had real

snow on the floor instead of just white confetti. Not so great for dancing, but it would have looked wonderful." Gina was just chattering to fill the space, trying to keep her voice airy and bright. She didn't want Dex to guess she was nervous as he pulled the car into a secluded spot overlooking the lake.

As Dex turned off the engine and slid his arm around her shoulders, panic coursed through Gina for a moment. He was going to kiss her. As she closed her eyes and waited for his lips to meet hers, she prayed that he'd never guess she hadn't been kissed as often as most seventeen-year-old girls.

But kissing, she realized as Dex's lips sweetly met her own, was like dancing. As long as her partner was good at what he was doing, she could follow his lead. His lips found hers like a magnet and guided her own, gently but insistently.

"You were right," he said hoarsely as he pulled back just slightly. "I should have asked you out before this. What was I wasting my time on a cold fish like Stacy Harcourt for when you were around?"

Then his lips touched hers again, moving with more intensity this time. Before long, Gina was wholeheartedly returning his kisses.

Gina was aware of a hundred incredible sensations at the same time: the softness of the skin on the back of Dex's neck under the fingers of her right hand, the rough wool weave of his jacket beneath her other hand, her own flesh tingling at the pressure of his hands sliding along the heavy velvet of her coat. She was content to stay like that for several minutes, drinking in Dex's warmth, his closeness, his sweet, soapy scent. Soon, Dex pulled Gina more tightly against him. "Ouch!" Gina yelped, jerking away and glaring at the gear shift that had just painfully crunched into her hipbone.

"That stupid shift! I knew I should have gotten an automatic!" Dex muttered furiously, slamming the shift with his hand. "Ouch!"

The spell of romance was abruptly shattered, and Gina found herself giggling as Dex started rubbing his injured palm. He switched his glare from the gear shift to her, but in a second he was laughing, too.

"Look!" Gina gestured toward the windshield, still chuckling. "We could be buried in snow, and we wouldn't even know it." The windshield was opaque with steam. "Dex, I really should get home," she added gently.

Dex was fumbling around beneath the seat.

"I could have sworn I had a rag here someplace. Got any tissues in your bag?"

Gina rummaged in her purse, producing two tissues that were unused and neatly folded. "Here you go," she said. "It looks like it's on the outside as well as in."

"Yeah. That's the snow I was so thrilled to see," Dex muttered. "I know I've got a scraper under here."

He finally located it and jumped out of the car. As he opened the door, Gina could see the snow was falling quite heavily. Enough had settled on the ground that it crunched under Dex's shoes.

As Dex circled the car, scraping the snow from the windows, Gina peeked at her wrist-watch. It was twelve-thirty!

She was more afraid of facing her parents than she was of the slippery winding roads leading away from the lake. She was glad Dex didn't want to talk when he returned to the car. He hunched over the wheel, peering intently at the snow-swept road stretching ahead, driving so slowly Gina knew he was worried about skidding.

For once, Gina wished they were going faster. Dex liked driving fast—she'd already seen that. If he was crawling, it meant he had no choice. But she couldn't forget the minutes dragging by, each one making her later. And her mother and father were waiting to meet her date! There was no question of introducing Dex to them when she was coming home an hour past curfew.

The sports car slid noiselessly into Marshall Road, and Gina saw with a sinking feeling that all the lights were on downstairs.

"I've got to get my shopping bag out of your trunk," she whispered, as if her parents could hear her behind the closed door fifty feet away.

"Right." His voice wasn't much louder than hers, and when he opened his door, he took care not to slam it shut, leaving the engine running and the hand brake on.

She was already standing on the curb when he opened the trunk. "Here you go, babe. Hope the folks don't come down on you too hard. I don't want a great night to end with a family feud."

"Oh, it won't," she said with a confidence she didn't feel. "I'd better run, though. I'll bet they're worried because of the snow. I had a great time, too."

"Next Friday, right? And, hey," he lowered his voice again. "If your folks hassle you, just tell them the car was acting up because of the weather. See you Monday." His lips barely brushed against hers as he hurried back around the car.

Gina's father had the front door open before she even reached it. "Gina! Where in the world have you been?" His voice was hoarse with worry, and it seemed to take a great effort on his part to keep from shouting. "Your mother was ready to call the hospitals!"

"Oh, Daddy, I'm really sorry!" she said passionately as she hurried into the warm foyer. "It was the car," she added in a rush of feeling. Guilt cut through her as she lied.

Gina's mother rushed in from the kitchen, wrapped in her old plaid flannel bathrobe, her hair hanging loose around her shoulders, her face pale and tight with worry. "Is that finally you?" she asked. "We were so worried, Gina! We couldn't imagine what might have happened. An accident! Anything! And you with a boy we don't even know!"

"It was the car," Gina repeated, more weakly this time. "It—it kept stalling all the time. Dex said that happens sometimes in the winter. Oh, I'm so sorry!" she wailed, close to tears as they stood in front of her, both looking so trusting and vulnerable. "I didn't mean to upset you so much! I promise it won't ever happen again!"

"Now, now, *bambina,* don't you get yourself all worked up, too." Her mother patted her shoulder. "You're here now, that's what counts."

"Right," Mr. Damone agreed as Gina's mother hugged her daughter to her side, stroking her hair the way she used to when Gina cried as a little girl. "You're safe and sound, and these accidents do happen. But where's Dex? He just dropped you off and drove away?"

"He didn't want to," Gina improvised, warned by a disapproving note in her father's voice. "He felt it was his duty to explain everything to you. But I knew his parents would be worrying, too, and I wasn't sure you'd be dressed for company."

He nodded slowly. "Yes, I can understand that. Well, now that you're home and we're all wide awake, why don't you put your coat in the closet and we'll all have a cup of cocoa? Just before I heard the car outside, your mama was going to make us some, weren't you, Magdalena?"

"The milk!" Mrs. Damone gasped, hurrying away. "I put it on to simmer and forgot it!"

"Now, you tell us all about the ball," Mr. Damone prompted Gina as he led her to the kitchen. "Did you have a good time?"

"Oh, it was wonderful!" Gina exclaimed ardently. "They took pictures for the newspaper, too!"

"You look beautiful in your new dress," her mother told her as she set three steaming mugs of cocoa on the table. "Doesn't she, Elio? And such a lovely corsage! But the poor flowers are crushed, Gina!"

"I guess I should have taken them off before I put my coat on," Gina mumbled, knowing the orchids had been smashed by Dex in the car. She realized her carnations were probably lying in a puddle of slush on the floor of the passenger's side. "Stacy got to be queen—we all knew she would—but I didn't care. Just being on the Court was so much fun."

She stopped to sip her cocoa. Her mother seemed to be studying her. Finally, Mrs. Damone said, "You look different tonight, so grown up. Perhaps it is your eyes?"

Gina remembered too late that she hadn't removed the makeup from her eyes. Her lipstick and blush had certainly been rubbed off in Dex's embrace.

"Um, Tess insisted on making them up for me," she said.

"She did a nice job," Mrs. Damone admitted

grudgingly. "For a big dance, I suppose it is permissible." She nodded.

"I couldn't be the only girl on the Court without makeup," Gina said defensively.

"And Dex?" her mother asked. "You enjoyed his company?"

"Oh, yes! I know you'll like him when you meet him," Gina insisted. "He already asked me to the movies next weekend. Can I go?" She looked pleadingly from her mother to her father. "We'd just go to the mall—I wouldn't be late."

Her mother's expression was doubtful, and Gina wanted to hug her father when he said slowly, "To the movies? I suppose there's no reason why not."

"Thank you," Gina said humbly. "And you can meet him then." Feeling suddenly exhausted, she stood up, stretching. "I should go to bed. It must be two o'clock."

"This has turned out to be a late night for all of us," her mother commented wearily. "We left the DiPietros' at ten."

"One thing, Gina," Mr. Damone said sharply as Gina turned to leave the room. "You tell Dex to have a mechanic take a good look at that car before you get in it again. Understand? This sort of thing cannot happen again."

"I'll tell him." She nodded. "I promise nothing like this will happen again. Honest!"

Dizzy with a mixture of relief and guilt, Gina scurried from the room. She didn't want to give her parents a chance to read the truth on her face.

THIRTEEN

"What a dead bunch!" Stacy muttered to Gina midway through Friday's pep rally, as the squad positioned itself for an old standby routine.

"Ms. Bowen was right about the fans losing their enthusiasm," Gina said, her voice dipping low in despair. "If everybody's as unenthusiastic as they sound right now, I'm afraid half the student body won't even bother going to the game tomorrow. Our bleachers are going to look pathetic!"

"Don't give up hope. This rally's not over yet," Stacy reminded her, "and we've still got your 'Blue and Gold' routine to get the old adrenaline pumping."

"Are you kidding? This crowd's so lifeless, I can't believe their *hearts* are even pumping," Gina retorted. But she was smiling as she ran to the center of the floor. This week, she knew, the cheerleaders were even more important than usual, because the team and the coaches were counting on them to get people excited about the following night's game.

"What if the whole routine just falls flat on its face?" Tess asked, as the squad huddled before its complex "Blue and Gold." "If we went to all that trouble to learn this and they just yawn, I think I'll burst out crying."

"Don't go getting mad at the kids, whatever you do," Stacy admonished. "Instead of blaming them for being apathetic, let's go out there and make 'em cheer!"

"Let's give it everything we got, guys!" Gina pushed every ounce of enthusiasm she possessed into her voice. "We'll *give* them all the spirit they need to show up tomorrow night and shout their lungs out!"

Gina's eyes scanned the bleachers anxiously as she joined the rest of the squad in spreading out across the floor and clapping out the rhythm of the routine.

The first few moves of the cheer were smooth, if not spectacular. Then came time for the real dancing. As Gina jumped to her feet from a split, she looked up and saw smiles and sparks of genuine interest in the crowd. Hands that had been stuck in jeans pockets suddenly began clapping in time. Gina grinned at Stacy. It looked as if this cheer might do the trick, after all!

The response built in intensity as the routine gained momentum, and Gina felt her own excitement and satisfaction growing. If only each of the six girls got through the double splits without a problem!

She couldn't see the others as she went into the first of the two splits, but she could feel them and hear them, and she knew they'd executed the move in perfect unison. Concentrating too intensely on her second split to look at the stands, Gina touched the floor, then pushed herself up.

A wave of cheers and applause greeted her, and she gasped with pleasure. The crowd continued to cheer as the squad left the floor and the coach's voice came on over the speakers to remind everyone to show up for the next night's game.

"We did it!" Stacy crowed as they headed for the locker room. "Listen to them yelling!"

"You were all great!" Gina congratulated them. "I'll bet a lot of people will show up at the game after all."

"Coming to Nicola's, Gina?" Patricia asked. "I'll drive you."

Gina agreed readily. Dex wasn't picking her up until eight. Too much free time would give her a chance to get nervous about introducing Dex to her parents.

"Have any plans tonight, Gina?" Patricia asked when they arrived at Nicola's.

"Dex is taking me to the movies out at the mall," Gina answered as coolly as she could, but she was sure her satisfaction at having a date with Dex showed.

"Dex Grantham!" Patricia sighed. "I think he's a real hunk. He's in one of my study halls, and I can't take my eyes off him."

"Any time you get tired of him, let me know," Sherri quipped.

"I never could figure out why Stacy got rid of him so fast," Patricia commented. "Not that Jeremy's not a doll."

"What makes you think Stacy got tired of him?" Gina asked knowingly. "I think Dex was the one who stopped asking her out."

"I suppose no one ever knows who got dumped in those flash-in-the-pan relationships," Sherri interrupted. "Some people's chemistry just clashes, I suppose."

"Not like you and Todd, huh?" Gina teased.

Sherri's delicate complexion deepened. "I really like him. And I think he likes me, too. We're going to see that new movie, *Fire Lake*."

"That's where Dex and I are going," Gina said. "The eight-thirty show? I'll look for you. Maybe we can all sit together."

As Gina opened the front door to her house later that afternoon, the rich, heavy aroma of roasting beef rushed to meet her. Normally, just the scent of roast beef would have been enough to entice her, but this time the thought of food made her nervous stomach queasy. She'd have to fake it at dinner. To her mother, having no appetite meant an impending illness, and if Gina said she wasn't hungry, she'd find herself tucked into bed with a thermometer between her lips.

She hung up her coat, practiced a few smiles in the hall mirror, then headed for the kitchen, cheerily announcing, "Hi, I'm home! And something smells yummy!" Beneath her smiling mask, she chided herself for failing to try out for any of the school plays. Acting, it seemed, came as naturally to her as dancing.

FOURTEEN

"Oh, Dex, you say the funniest things! You're really a riot. I've never—" Gina stopped short. "Oh, no, that sounds pathetic!"

Wrapped in a big terry-cloth towel, Gina glared at her reflection in the steamy bathroom mirror. If she talked to Dex like that, he'd think she had lost her mind.

"Hey, Gina, are you going to hog the bathroom all night?" Dino demanded from the hallway. "Who're you talking to, anyhow?"

Putting on her robe and gathering her belongings, Gina flung open the door. "All yours," she said coolly as she marched past her little brother. "And for your information, I was just practicing one of tomorrow's cheers." She hurried into her room and closed the door before he could say anything else.

She continued to try new remarks as she

dried her hair and dressed, finally deciding to forget the whole thing. Anything she rehearsed *sounded* rehearsed.

When Dex rang the front bell, she was waiting for him in the living room with her parents. *We look almost like a normal American family,* she told herself just as the bell rang. Gina wore navy corduroy slacks and a green-and-blue-striped sweater. Her mother wore a new dress she had bought the day they picked out Gina's formal, while Mr. Damone's tan corduroy jacket hid the suspenders that hitched up his camel trousers, making him look like any other college professor.

Dex, in a down ski jacket, crewneck sweater, and gray flannels, looked like the boy every parent would choose as a daughter's date. "Hi, Dex," she said. "Come on in and meet my parents."

"I can hardly wait," he muttered, but he winked as he spoke.

It all went better than Gina had imagined. Dex was so soft-spoken and polite, it was hard to imagine he was the same guy who made so many wisecracks at school.

"I take it you've had your car checked out," Mr. Damone said sternly.

"It's running like a top now, sir," Dex said smoothly, avoiding an outright lie.

"Don't forget, Gina"—her father's words followed Gina and Dex down the walk as they left—"home by twelve o'clock."

"Midnight!" Dex exclaimed when they reached the car. "Boy, your parents are real swingers, aren't they? I thought you didn't have a curfew."

"They're usually not so strict," she fibbed. "I guess I'm sort of on probation because of coming in so late last week and worrying them."

"Well, at least it's not a three-hour movie," he said grudgingly as they drove away.

On the way to the mall, Gina tried to begin a conversation, but nothing came to her mind or her lips. All she could think about was the disastrous first impression her parents had ended up making on Dex.

Not until they'd parked in the lot and were walking toward the block of four tiny theaters did Gina manage to say, "I told Sherri Callahan we'd look for her. She's coming tonight with Todd."

"Lots of kids won't be coming till the *later* show," Dex said pointedly, as if to make sure Gina knew nobody else had such a childish curfew.

All four theaters shared the same box office, so it wasn't surprising that the line for tickets was so long it stretched almost to the main part of the mall. But Dex sounded disgusted as he grumbled, "Great, nine million people are here already. And we can't go to the *later* show. You can stand and wait if you want, not me. Come on, let's go to the hot dog stand down at the end of the mall and grab a Coke or something. Maybe the line will be gone when we're finished."

Gina sighed. A promising evening had turned bad already. Dex was clearly annoyed that she had such strict rules to follow.

As they approached the snack bar, Gina nodded to Tif Rafferty and her date, who were sharing a paper plate of French fries. She wasn't thrilled at the prospect of talking to them, but she was glad to see Dex's expression brighten as he headed their way. At least he was smiling again.

As far as Gina was concerned, Tif's date, Howie Fellows, was a pain in the neck. She couldn't find fault with Howie's looks, which were probably Tif's main concern. But good looks didn't make up for his crude jokes and mean cracks about kids who didn't meet his harsh social standards. Gina knew that Dex and

Howie were friends, but she couldn't believe it would last very long once Dex found out what Howie was really like.

Gina was glad when Howie announced he and Tif were seeing a different movie than the one she and Dex were going to. "This time of year, nothing beats watching those chicks run around on the screen in little bikinis, right, man?" He poked Dex in the ribs and arched his eyebrows.

Tif sat silently while the two boys exchanged wisecracks and tried to out-boast each other. Gina followed Tif's lead, smiling and sipping her soda.

Gina began to worry that they would miss the opening of the movie when she spotted Tony Genovese.

He was with another guy, and as his eyes met Gina's he smiled widely and headed her way. "Hey, Gina! Long time no see!"

"Hi, Tony," Gina said. She was so surprised at running into him outside one of their familiar gatherings that she just smiled, not saying anything more for a minute. Then she realized conversation at the table had stopped. "Oh, sorry," she apologized. "Tony Genovese, this is Dex Grantham and Tif Rafferty and Howie Fellows."

"Hi." Tony nodded. "This is my buddy Carmine Rocco." He introduced his friend. "You going to the movies?"

Gina nodded. "We're going to see *Fire Lake*. There's supposed to be lots of good music."

"That's what we just saw. It's terrific. Good acting, too. But you'd better get in line or you'll be stuck in the first row."

"I guess we should get going," Gina agreed, looking at her watch. "The movie starts in five minutes," she said to Dex.

"You going to come by tomorrow night?" Tony asked as Gina set down her empty paper cup. "My mom keeps asking about you."

"Not tomorrow, Tony. But soon," Gina promised. "Tell everyone I said hello, okay?"

No sooner had the two couples turned the corner toward the box office than Howie started snickering. "Is that guy for real? His *mom* keeps asking about you? What do you do, Gina, babysit for him?"

"His mother's a friend of my family's," Gina said stiffly, wondering why Tif and Dex were laughing.

"Hey, don't get uptight," Dex said. "Howie's only kidding, aren't you, man? He's just feeling left out 'cause he doesn't have a friend with a girl's name, right, Howie?"

"No joke, I think I'll change my name to something classy like Carmen. How about Mimi . . . or Tootsie?" Howie pushed his voice into a broken falsetto. "Hi, I'm Carmen, and this is my friend Fifi."

Gina's chest tightened, and she started to explain that his name was Carmine and not Carmen and that it was a perfectly acceptable Italian man's name. But Dex had already called her uptight. She managed to laugh along with the others. And she nodded when Dex chuckled again as they entered the theater and said, "Man, Howie's really a riot, isn't he?"

Dex and Gina had spent so much time talking to Howie and Tif that the only seats left were in the third row. At least the movie was as good as Tony had said, and the warmth of Dex's arm around her shoulders helped Gina ignore the stiff neck she was getting from craning to see the screen.

Only when the film ended and the lights went up did Gina remember her promise to sit with Sherri and Todd. "I completely forgot about telling Sherri we'd sit together!" she exclaimed, standing and scanning the crowd, but they were nowhere in sight.

"I feel terrible," Gina said.

"Hey, babe, don't worry about it," Dex told

her. "They were supposed to save us seats, right?"

Gina fought an urge to point out that she and Dex had arrived just as the movie was beginning.

After the movies, she and Dex went to Nicola's, where they were greeted enthusiastically. Gina usually felt awkward and shy at Nicola's if she wasn't surrounded by the rest of the cheering squad, but tonight she found herself making small talk with an ease that both surprised and delighted her. The kids from Midvale were acting friendlier, and she knew why. Dex Grantham had given her his seal of approval by taking her to the Winter Carnival Ball.

It wasn't as if she hadn't been popular before. She was cocaptain of the cheerleading squad. But in the past, Gina had never had the kind of easy rapport with all the kids at school that someone like Tess seemed to have.

With Dex by her side, conversation came easy for her. Kim Belford, a junior varsity cheerleader, couldn't say enough about the varsity squad's new cheer. Kim told Gina how professional the choreography had looked and that all the JV cheerleaders were envious of the new routine.

"Why don't you talk to the rest of your squad and see if they'd like me and Stacy to help you work something up sometime?" Gina offered.

"Do you mean it?" Kim asked eagerly. "You'd actually be willing to coach a bunch of freshmen and sophomores?"

"Sure I would. And I'm sure Stacy would, too." Gina made a mental note to talk to Stacy about it.

The time passed so quickly that Gina forgot to be nervous around Dex. Her confidence momentarily left her when she saw it was a quarter to twelve. But Dex spared her the embarrassment of reminding him it was time for her to leave. He turned to her and said, "Hey, Cinderella, I'd better deliver you straight to your door if I want your parents to let you go out with me again."

When Dex pulled up in front of her house, he asked her out for the following weekend even before he pulled her toward him and covered her lips with his own. She knew then he had recovered from his earlier anger about her curfew.

When she slipped into bed a half hour later, Gina was still tingling with the memory of Dex's kisses. She could hardly believe it was true. She was dating Dex Grantham, and he didn't even seem to care that she was not a tall, blond copy of Stacy Harcourt.

She lay on her back with her arms crossed beneath her head, eyes closed, playing back the scenes of the evening: Kim asking for her help, kids stopping by their booth at Nicola's to visit, Dex's arm draped around her shoulders at the movies. Then one image wiped the smile from her face: Dex and Tif and Howie laughing at Tony Genovese.

It's not as if Dex actually laughed at Tony, Gina told herself. *He was really laughing at Howie's goofing around. And I never really liked Howie, anyway.*

She was tired of trying to remember everything that had happened all night. Turning on her side, she snuggled into her pillow and fell into a deep sleep.

FIFTEEN

In spite of a surprisingly large turnout at Saturday's game against Brownville, the Mustangs lost. For the next two weeks, Gina and the rest of the squad devoted themselves to boosting school spirit. The Mustangs had to fight hard to make it to the semifinals.

Gina's life had settled into a routine of cheering, talking and exchanging advice with Tess and Stacy, and dating Dex—a routine she once had daydreamed about. By the time she'd been dating Dex for a month, most people took it for granted that they were a couple. "Meeting Dex after class?" Valerie would ask if she and Tif caught up with Gina on the way to history.

Afternoons when the squad didn't practice, Gina would sit in a booth at Nicola's with Stacy and Tess, joined by Marsha or Julie or Janet or someone else from their class. She spent several Saturdays with Tess, helping her decide what clothes and books to pack and what to give away.

The first week of March blew in with chilling force. Gina had learned to accept Midwestern weather—an endless winter followed by the unbroken heat of summer. When she arrived at Tess's house the first Saturday morning in March, she was chilled in spite of her down coat and heavy clothes, and she plunged into the front hall as soon as Tess opened the door.

"Brrr, it's like the Ice Age out there!" she gasped, pulling off her mittens and rubbing her hands together to keep them warm.

"You should have told me you were walking," Tess chided her, taking her coat and hanging it on the oak clothes tree. "I'd have picked you up."

"I didn't think I'd catch frostbite in six short blocks," Gina answered. "Is my nose still there? I can't feel anything."

Tess narrowed her eyes. "Didn't it used to be in the center of your face?" She shook her head sadly. "Just an ice slick now."

"You can twist my arm and force me to take a ride home, okay?"

"Come to my room and see if you want anything I'm tossing out." Tess led the way. "Mom and I drove out to look at the models at Clover Farms this morning, and let me tell you, there's not room for so much as a spare lipstick in those townhouses!"

"You don't sound too down about it," Gina observed.

Tess shrugged, flopping on one of the twin beds and turning down the blaring stereo. "No use crying over spilt milk, right? It turns out my cousin and her husband will definitely buy this place, so the minute the divorce comes through, we're moving. I don't know, maybe it won't be so bad. The main bathroom has a built-in make-up table, the kind with lights around the mirror like a movie star's dressing room. And Mom says we can get a puppy! I always wanted one, but since Dad's allergic . . . Anyhow, why don't you take a look through those." She gestured toward two shoeboxes on the other bed.

Gina sat down and started going through the contents—both boxes were filled to the brim with eye shadows, lip liners and glosses, pow-ders, and blushes. "How did you ever end up with so much makeup?" Gina asked in amazement. "I've never seen so many different colors outside a drugstore!"

"And that's only what I'm throwing out," Tess reminded her. "I should probably keep it all forever to remind myself how much money I wasted on the stuff. Like that blusher you just picked up. Wait'll you open it."

"Yuck! Iridescent fuchsia? Whatever made you buy this?"

"That was my *Flashdance* period," Tess said ruefully. "I gave Mom all my torn jerseys months ago to use as dustcloths. You should have seen me with that blusher on! I looked like the Bride of Frankenstein."

"Not for me, thanks." Gina dropped the plastic container back into the box.

"What did you and Dex do last night?"

Gina wrinkled her nose. "Went over to Howie Fellows's house and watched some old movies on his VCR."

"You don't sound like you had such a great time," Tess commented.

Gina looked at her friend, who'd propped herself up on one elbow and was looking at her curiously. "Oh, it was all right. The movies were great—the Marx Brothers in *Duck Soup* and Woody Allen's *Sleeper*. I just get bored with

Howie sometimes, you know? I don't know why Dex thinks he's so great."

"They're alike in a lot of ways, aren't they?"

"Dex and Howie?" Gina's voice rose. "Not at all. Howie's loud and obnoxious and rude. You should have seen the way his mother waited on him hand and foot. No wonder he's such a spoiled brat. What did you and Dave do?"

"Sat around the dining room table doing homework. Romantic, huh? He's way behind with his trig because of basketball, and I've got a French quiz coming up Monday, so we both thought we should just hit the books for a change. We're going to Mary Bowes's party after next week's game, though. Two weekends of studying in a row is too much!"

"Yeah, I suppose we'll go, too," Gina murmured absently as she continued to look over Tess's discarded makeup, putting aside the few things she thought she might use.

"You and Grantham are really an item, aren't you?" Tess asked. "I mean, he's had more dates with you than with any other girl I can remember."

"I guess we are," Gina said simply. She wondered what Tess would say if she told her she didn't feel like Dex's girlfriend, not when she was alone with him, anyway. Around school, around other kids, she felt as if she had acquired new status. She enjoyed that. After all, you got to know new people when you were part of a couple, and having a boyfriend who was both popular and handsome seemed to make some kids friendlier to her.

But Gina didn't feel she knew Dex any better after weeks of dating than she had the night of the Winter Carnival Ball. When she tried to talk to him about how he felt or what he was thinking, he made a joke or changed the subject. Maybe she was just expecting too much too soon. She knew a hundred girls would happily trade places with her. Maybe she was just as uptight as Dex said. According to him, she was uptight when she didn't laugh at Howie Fellows's remarks; she was uptight when she removed his hand from her sweater when they parked by the lake; she was uptight when she reminded him it was time to go home.

As much as she could, Gina gave in. She forced a smile to her lips when Howie said something everybody else thought was funny. She stayed in Dex's embrace even though it meant getting home fifteen minutes late. She even let him talk her into telling her parents she had a special practice so they could go to the movies on a weeknight, when she wasn't allowed to date.

All Gina had to do was look at Dex to know she didn't want anyone else. And when she caught a reflection of the two of them in a mirror, the sight was still enough to take her breath away: Gina Damone and Dex Grantham, the all-American couple.

"Gina, are you going out tonight?" Tess called her from her reverie.

Gina shook her head. "Mom and Dad are having some friends over, so I'm staying in."

"Well, if you get bored, give me a call. You can help me think up a name for my dog."

"But you haven't even gotten it yet," Gina reminded her.

"I know, but I know just what I want: a little raggedy Benji sort of puppy. That shouldn't be hard to find at the pound. And I think it'll be nice for him to have a name as soon as he comes home."

"What about 'Passionate Plum'?" Gina read the label on the bottom of a tube of lipstick. "That's got a catchy ring to it." She giggled. "Or 'Untamed Desire Peach'? Really, Tess, I'd be embarrassed even to ask for some of these things in the store!"

"Some help you are!" Tess grabbed a pillow and hurled it at the other bed. "Come on, let's go raid the icebox. I haven't eaten since nine, and I'm starving!"

Yes, I am uptight, Gina thought after Tess had dropped her off. Tess took things as they came and laughed about them; Gina fretted about them.

"Would you describe me as an uptight person?" she asked Tony Genovese that night as they sat over the Trivial Pursuit board he'd brought along.

He looked up. Under the harsh fluorescent lighting of the Damones' kitchen, his features were gently amused. "Uptight? What makes you ask that—the fact that I've got a green, an orange, and a brown chip, and you've only got one pink one?"

"No, silly, I'm being serious!" she insisted, but she was smiling in spite of herself. Tony was even cuter than Dino at times, like a mischievous little boy instead of a high school senior. "Do you think I have a hard time letting myself go?"

"I always have fun when I'm with you, Gina," he said, his tone more serious. "You know, I wish—"

"You wish what?" she prompted him when he didn't go on.

He shrugged. "I wish you weren't always so hard on yourself," he answered. "Where did you get the idea you were uptight? That guy you've been dating giving you a hard time?"

"Dex really isn't so bad, Tony. Honest. I'm sure you'd like him if you got to know him. What did you meet him for—thirty seconds out at the mall?"

"Thirty seconds was enough time for me to get the feeling we wouldn't like each other," Tony said stiffly. "The guy just rubbed me the wrong way."

Gina flushed, remembering how Howie and Dex had laughed at Carmine's name. "Dex likes to laugh at everything," she argued. "Things, not people."

"Don't you think there's a little more to life than having a lot of laughs?"

"Oh, stop sounding like such a stick in the mud, Tony! You're almost as bad as my folks."

"See?" he said, his voice tight. "You don't have to worry about being uptight. *I'm* the one who's uptight, right? Me and your parents." He pushed the die across the board to her. "Go ahead, it's your turn."

She shook the die and let it go, unable to think of what to say, knowing that she'd hurt Tony. She hadn't meant to, but it was true that he was more like her folks than like Dex. And that meant he belonged to a world that was too old-fashioned for Gina.

SIXTEEN

The days that followed were even colder than the weekend had been. By Wednesday, the thermometer had dropped to ten degrees and people were arriving at school swaddled in scarves, hoods, and mittens.

In that day's history class, Gina was too busy admiring Dex's profile to take legible notes. She went to her room after dinner and was trying to reconstruct her notes when her brother banged on her closed door.

"Telephone, Gina. Mom says it's Dex," he trilled.

Gina grabbed the extension phone from her parents' room, passing Dino still outside her door on the way back. "You're not planning to stand here and eavesdrop, are you?" she asked threateningly.

"Boy, I really care what mushy things you

two have to say to each other." He snorted to show his disgust, then headed for the stairway.

"Hope the blades are sharpened on your ice skates," were Dex's first words when Gina picked up the phone. "Brinton's Lake has finally frozen over."

"It's about time! I was starting to wonder if winter was going to end with no ice-skating!" Gina sank down cross-legged on her bed, smiling with satisfaction. She loved ice-skating, but this year's cycle of freezes and thaws had kept the lake from freezing solid from December to February. "I hope there's not a thaw before the weekend."

"Forget the weekend," Dex said. "The important thing is it's frozen now. Skating starts tonight!"

"Tonight? What do you mean?"

"There's a big party planned for tonight at midnight, Gina. There's a full moon, too, so it won't even be dark. We'll have a blast."

"Not me, Dex," she said quickly. "I wish I could, but you know how my folks are about letting me go out during the week. They'd never give me permission to go ice-skating on a weeknight. And certainly not at midnight. Even *they* go to bed before midnight during the week."

"That's fine, then," he answered. "If they're already asleep, they'll never have to know you're going anyplace."

"You're crazy!" Gina laughed shakily, hoping Dex was kidding. "I can't sneak out."

Silence greeted her protest. Dex wasn't kidding at all. She was about to ask if he was still there when he spoke again, his voice cold.

"What is it with you, Gina? Are you going to let your parents keep you from ever having a good time? I'm getting sick of all these rules and regulations."

"Look, I know my folks are strict, but do you think most people would let their kids go to a party at midnight on a school night?"

"Not every night of the week," Dex answered. "But this is a special occasion. We've been waiting months for the lake to freeze."

Gina sighed. "I can't, Dex. I just can't. I know they'd say no if I asked them, and I can't sneak out."

"All right, if that's how you feel," he said, icicles dripping from his voice. "If you want to miss a party everyone else is going to be at, I know Valerie's been pretty bored since she stopped going out with Cal. I'm sure she'd like to go with me."

"Wait! You mean you'd take Valerie Masters

just because I'm not allowed to go?" she asked tightly, not sure whether to be angry or hurt.

Dex's voice softened. "It's not like I *want* to go with Val, Gina. You know that. I want to go with you. I mean, you're my girl, aren't you?"

"Am I?" It was the closest Dex had ever come to saying he cared about her.

"Of course you are, babe," he murmured, his voice low and seductive now. "You're the only girl I want to be with. But I can't show up at the lake without a date, not when everybody in school's going to be there. If I show up alone, they'll all start mocking me. You should hear the way they go on when I walk into Nicola's at twelve-thirty all by myself. 'Where's Cinderella, Grantham? Get her home all safe and sound?' Maybe you don't mind being a joke, Gina, but I do."

She felt herself go cold all over, then hot. Why hadn't Dex told her before this that all the kids laughed about her curfew? She should have known her parents would eventually ruin everything for her. "I didn't know—" she began.

"Listen, Gina, why don't you just let yourself go for a change, huh? We don't have to stay long. We can get there, skate for a while and get back, and your folks'll never know you're gone. What's the big deal?"

"Well, if everyone else is really going to be there—"

"Look, I'll pick you up on your corner at about ten to twelve, all right?"

Gina hesitated. She knew she should say no. If the lake was still frozen by the weekend, then she could skate. If not, those were the breaks. But Dex's attitude had made his intentions clear: if she wasn't willing to bend the rules, he'd find someone who wasn't so uptight. And the picture of everyone in her class laughing because she wasn't allowed to do all the things they took for granted wasn't a pretty one.

She sighed. "All right," she agreed reluctantly. "But you promise we don't have to stay long?"

"Promise. Just wait, we'll have a great time, Gina."

She hung up, then took the phone back to her parents' room. In her own bedroom again, she rooted through her closet until she found her skates. She wondered if the other girls would be wearing skating skirts, then decided it would be too cold on the lake at midnight to wear anything but jeans and a heavy sweater.

When she'd hung up the phone, Gina had felt she was making the right decision. But as the minutes ticked away on the clock next to her bed, she had second thoughts. She realized too late that she should have phoned Tess to make sure she and Dave were going. Now it was too late to disturb Mrs. Belding. But Dex had seemed pretty definite when he'd said everyone would be there, and Gina was tired of being on the outside looking in, missing events because of her parents.

At ten-thirty she went downstairs and made herself a cup of cocoa, making a big show of yawning and saying good night to her mother and father. In the bathroom, she brushed her teeth and washed her face, but she put on fresh makeup when she'd finished, and instead of changing into her pajamas she crawled beneath the covers dressed in her jeans, heavy socks, and a heavy wool sweater with a cotton turtle-neck underneath.

The luminous numbers on the bedside clock showed it was eleven-fifteen when she heard her parents go to bed, but she still didn't move. She waited fifteen more minutes, until the house was completely dark and quiet, before leaving her bed.

Gina made her way down the stairs in the dim glow of the hall night-light, holding her skates close to her chest so they wouldn't swing out and thud against the wall.

She pulled on her jacket, checked her purse twice to make sure she had her front door key, then took a deep breath and let herself out the door, pulling it closed carefully and quietly behind her.

The street was still and deserted, although lights burned behind several windows. The moon above was round and bright. Gina had no trouble seeing as she made her way down the path to the sidewalk.

When she reached the corner, she stepped off the sidewalk and out of the light thrown from the street lamp. Her skates slung over one shoulder, she dug her mittened hands deep into her jacket pockets, peering up and down the street as if that would make Dex arrive sooner.

Gina half hoped Dex would stand her up. Then she'd be able to slip quietly back into the house and her bed and forget this whole plan. Still, in spite of her apprehension, Gina's heart beat fast from excitement as well as fear. She'd never been to a midnight party before.

When she spotted Dex's car heading toward her from a block away, she stepped into the sidewalk's circle of light.

"You can just throw your skates behind the seat," he told her, his voice low, as she jumped in the car and locked the door. He didn't give her a chance to fasten her seat belt before he accelerated, leaving the familiar neighborhood streets far behind.

"Who's going to be there?" Gina asked as Dex turned onto the highway that led to the lake.

"All sorts of people," he answered impatiently. "I told you everybody's going, Gina. What did you expect me to do, get a guest list?"

"I was just asking," she protested.

"Look, you'll have a good time, all right?" Dex said shortly, and she resolved not to ask any more questions. He was clearly still annoyed with her for having hesitated to come when he'd first asked her.

Instead of turning down the road where they usually went to the park, Dex stayed on the highway that led to the far side of the lake. There was an old pavilion on this side, as well as a place called the Lake Shore Tavern, a rundown bar that was busy in the summer when the cottages on the shore were filled with vacationers.

As Dex parked the car on the edge of the tavern lot, Gina could see bonfires along the lake's edge and the silhouettes of skaters already on the ice.

"I'll grab the skates," Dex said as Gina

climbed out, almost losing her balance when the leather soles of her loafers made contact with the icy pavement.

Gina took the skates Dex held out to her as they gingerly made their way across the frozen earth to the lake, her eyes combing the darkness as she tried to discern familiar faces ahead of her.

"Dex?" she said as they approached the edge of the ice. "I don't see anyone from school."

He made no effort to hide his exasperation. "Lighten up, would you?"

"Hey, Dex! Over here!" someone called from about twenty feet farther along the shore. Her eyes had grown accustomed to the dark, and Gina recognized Mark, Dex's brother.

"Wasn't sure you were going to make it," Mark said as Gina and Dex came alongside the log on which he was perched.

"Hey, man, me miss a party? You know better than that!" Dex laughed. "You know Gina Damone?"

"Yeah, sure. You were a JV cheerleader the year I graduated, right? And your dad is Professor Damone?" Mark asked offhandedly. Turning back to Dex, he said, "Grab yourself a piece of log. We just sent Dave Schultz into the tavern to get a couple of six-packs of brew. Ted and Larry and Stew and the rest of the guys are around here someplace."

"Where's everyone from school, Dex?" Gina asked as calmly as she could. "I thought you said they would be here!"

"Cool it, would you?" he muttered angrily. "Look, here comes Howie."

Howie Fellows was arriving from behind the shadows of the pavilion, but Gina hardly considered him "everyone" from Midvale.

"Hey, way to go, my man!" Howie said raucously as he came up alongside them. "This is great! Sure your brother doesn't mind us crashing his frat party, though?"

"Nah. Mark's right over there. Why don't you go say hi?" Dex answered as Gina stiffened beside him.

"Frat party? Dex, I thought you said all the kids from school were going to be here!"

"So I was wrong." He shrugged. "Big deal. Look, here comes Dave. Why don't you just loosen up and have a beer? Why do you have to be so uptight all the time?"

Gina blinked back tears of shock and anger as Dex stood and walked over to the spot where a guy carrying two six-packs of beer was joining Mark and Howie and a few older guys. She couldn't believe that Dex had lied to her even though he knew what a risk it was for her to sneak out. But that was exactly what he'd done. Howie was obviously the only other person from school who'd be at Brinton's Lake.

Dex trudged back over, a beer can in each hand. "Here," he said, holding one out to her.

"I don't want that!" she told him, her voice low but furious. "I don't drink beer. And I don't think you should either, Dex." She got to her feet. "What I do think is that you should take me back home right now."

"You want to leave, go ahead," Dex said in a voice as cold as the ice on the lake. "But I'm going to stay and have some fun." He gestured toward a bunch of particularly loud and obnoxious guys to their left. "I'm sure one of Mark's fraternity brothers over there would be glad to give you a lift."

The smirk on his face infuriated Gina. But it frightened her a little, too. "Come on, knock it off, would you?" she said. "I don't think any of this is very funny, Dex. I—"

"Nobody's keeping you here," he said, then turned and walked away. As he plopped himself down on the log next to his brother and started pulling on his skates, the awful truth finally hit Gina. He was serious! Dex had no intention of driving her back home now. She was stranded.

With trembling fingers, she pawed through her purse and found her wallet. It contained just what she'd been afraid of: two dollar bills and assorted change, not enough for a taxi even if she could get one to pick her up. She was afraid to ask any of the older guys for a ride home, and she knew it was useless to expect Howie to help. Howie would never do anything to displease Dex. She sighed, blinking back her tears as she thrust her wallet back into her bag. She could wait and hope Dex got bored soon, but what if he decided to stay out all night?

Gina could hardly call her parents, who'd be so mad she wouldn't blame them if they sent a squad car for her. Even if she were willing to confess her stupidity to any of the girls from school, they'd all be asleep. It was all too clear that, no matter what Dex had told her, all the other girls had curfews and rules just as she did.

For a few minutes Gina sat on the log, watching Dex as he clowned with Mark and Howie on the ice. He looked just as handsome as usual, his dark hair slightly mussed, his features regular, his tailored clothes fitting him perfectly. Though she was numb with the knowledge of his selfishness, Gina couldn't hate Dex. He had led her on about the skating party, but if she'd been stronger she would have said no. She'd been awfully easy to convince.

Grabbing her skates and her bag, Gina rose and walked reluctantly toward the tavern, a low bungalow with peeling gray paint and a flickering neon sign that proclaimed, "L KE S ORE AVE N." She dreaded going inside, but she knew she had to. Only one person could save her now. And if Tony Genovese wouldn't agree to help her, she didn't know what she'd do.

SEVENTEEN

Gina tried to look tall and fearless as she dropped a quarter into the pay phone in one corner of the bar. The place gave her the creeps, but she knew it wasn't a good idea to look frightened.

The barroom smelled of spilled beer and stale cigarette smoke. Except for Gina, only two burly guys sat in the tavern. Luckily for her, they were too busy watching the female bartender to notice the girl who'd scurried inside and made a dash for the phone on the wall.

She had to look up Tony's number in her little cloth-covered phone book. Now she dialed the seven digits with clumsy fingers, hoping Tony would be the one to answer the phone. She knew it was in the hall next to his bedroom.

When his familiar voice mumbled a sleepy hello, her legs threatened to buckle under her in relief. She found her own voice and managed to blurt a shorthand version of what had happened.

"Just tell me where to pick you up, Gina," Tony said.

"Okay, I'll come right out," he said when she'd finished. "You know it's going to take me almost twenty minutes to get there, though. Why don't you lock yourself in the ladies' room for fifteen minutes, then go outside. Stand right by the front door in the light, all right?"

"All right," she agreed. He hung up before she could say anything else.

A red Firebird roared into the lot as soon as Gina stepped outside fifteen minutes later. She could see by the set of Tony's jaw that he was furious. She wondered for a panicked moment if Tony was going to embarrass her by confronting Dex. But he pulled out of the lot and onto the highway as soon as she closed the door behind her.

"I really appreciate your coming out like this," she told him, giddy with relief. "I couldn't believe Dex would really just leave me stranded like this, not when he knew I shouldn't have been here in the first place."

"So how come you're here then?" he asked abruptly. "It's not as if he held a gun to your head and made you come. What made you agree to do something so stupid—and so sneaky?"

It dawned on Gina that Tony was angry not with Dex, but with her. "It's not fair to pick on me!" she protested. "Okay, so I shouldn't have done it. But you don't know what it's like having parents like mine. He was always mocking me for having to be home so early whenever we went out, and he insisted everybody from school was going to be there tonight. I believed him when he said the other girls would be allowed out because it was a special party!"

"You mean you listened to him because he told you what you wanted to hear," Tony insisted.

"That's not true," she protested. "Well, maybe it is, but so what? Dex is right. Okay, maybe the other kids don't have as much freedom to come and go as he tried to make out they did. But they're not stuck with weird parents who don't understand anything about life in America, either!"

Instead of softening, his voice was harsh as he said, "It sounds to me like your parents understand more about America than you do, Gina. At least they understand the important thing."

"What's that?" she asked.

He didn't take his eyes off the road as he answered. "They understand that in this country everyone's free to be different if they want. That's why so many people want to come here, isn't it? That's why your parents and my parents came here, and because they did, you and I are better off than we'd be back in Italy. But you won't let them be themselves, Gina. You're so ashamed of little things like your father's suspenders that you don't even give them a chance."

"What do you mean, I don't give them a chance?" she asked defensively. "A chance at what?"

"I've overheard things your mom tells mine," Tony retorted. "'Gina says nobody's parents go to Career Night.' 'Gina says the games are for the students and not the parents.' How do you expect them to understand when you cut them off from everything and keep them in the dark? Do you ever bring your friends home from school or invite them over to hang out?"

"No," she admitted. "But they *wouldn't* understand, Tony. And if I talked them into going to things at school, what good would it do? People would just laugh at them, the way my father's students at the university laugh at him."

"What makes you think that?" he asked, sounding genuinely surprised. "A couple of my friends are taking your father's course at school, and he's supposed to be the most popular teacher in the engineering school. Nobody thinks he's a joke. The students worship him."

"I'll bet," Gina said sarcastically. "Anyhow, going to Career Night wouldn't suddenly make them agree to let me study dancing. To them, it's college, college, college."

"Why can't you go to college and minor in dance?" he asked. "Can't you compromise?"

"You just don't know what they're like, Tony," she argued. "They hated when I cut my hair, they don't like me wearing makeup, they think eleven o'clock is late! They'd never let me be like everyone else."

"Have you really tried to tell them your friends don't live by such strict rules?"

"No. What's the use?" she asked angrily. "I'd just be wasting my time."

"I suppose you think Dino's wasting his time when he does things to show your mom he's proud of her," Tony retorted.

"Does things? What's he done?"

"You didn't even know he asked her to

come and talk to his fourth-grade class about going to night school?" Tony asked. "I guess you wouldn't. Have you ever thought about how hard your mom's working, holding down a job and going to night school, too, just so she can get a diploma? Instead of being proud of her, you're probably afraid the kids at Midvale will find out she didn't graduate from high school a long time ago, right?"

"You make me sound so awful, Tony!" Gina exclaimed, her voice shaking. "If anybody heard you, they'd think you were on their side and not mine."

"Why do there have to be two sides?" he asked with maddening calmness. "Why do you have to see your folks as the enemy?"

"They're certainly not my allies," she told him smartly. "Not the way they shoot down any chances I have of fitting in."

They were on Marshall Road now, and Tony coasted to a stop along the curb a few doors down from the Damones' house. "Who are your allies then?" he asked coolly. "Creeps like Dex Grantham who don't even treat you with respect?"

"That's not true!" Gina's voice rang with feeling. Though she would never have imagined this evening would end with her sticking up for

Dex, Tony's know-it-all attitude was making her defensive. "Maybe Dex did act like a real rat tonight, but he's not always like that."

"I suppose he's a real prince when you get to know him!" Tony snorted contemptuously.

"Dex happens to be one of the most popular guys in the entire school," Gina said primly. "You don't know anything about him."

"I can't believe this!" Tony smacked himself on the forehead. "I must be hearing things, because you can't really be sticking up for that jerk after what he did to you tonight. You wake me up in the middle of the night, drag me out of bed to save you from him, then start telling me how popular he is? What's your problem, Gina?"

"I don't have a problem," she said stiffly. "I appreciate your picking me up. But that doesn't mean you've got the right to lecture me about my parents and my taste in men."

"What taste in men?" He laughed grimly. "If you mean that Dex Grantham, then you haven't got any taste in men at all. If you have anything to do with him ever again, you're the biggest fool in the world."

"Would you just get off my case?" she muttered through clenched teeth. "I don't know if I'm going to keep on seeing Dex or not, it so happens. But that's my concern, isn't it? Or do you think it would serve me right if I didn't have another date until graduation?"

"Who said anything about not having another date? You wouldn't have to sit home weekends just because you gave Dex a big kick out of your life, you know."

"Oh, yeah? And how do you know that? How do you know I'd ever get asked out again?"

"Because I'd ask you!" he all but shouted, turning to face her, his eyes fiery.

"*You* would?" she whispered.

"Of course I would!" he said, sounding angry all over again. "I almost did a couple of times before you got hooked up with that—that creep! Only, you never gave me a chance."

"But I didn't—"

"No, of course you didn't know! I'm sure it never occurred to you that good old Tony might be interested in you. But then, I'm not your type, am I? A little old-fashioned for your taste, huh?" He gasped exaggeratedly. "Gina Damone date Tony Genovese? Not on your life! Not when there are guys like Dex Grantham around." He sighed, running his fingers through his dark curls. "You're the one who doesn't understand, Gina," he said, sounding suddenly very tired. "You don't understand a thing."

She was too stunned to speak. Not that he

gave her a chance. "I can't sit here all night," he blurted, his voice jagged. "You'd better go sneak back in."

"But, Tony—" she began.

"We'll talk about it some other time." He cut her off, staring straight ahead now, avoiding her eyes. "I've got to get some sleep."

"I really do appreciate your coming out to get me," she said softly.

"No sweat." He shrugged. "Tony Genovese's always willing to help a damsel in distress."

He was still staring stonily in front of him as she gently eased the door open, slid out, and closed the door behind her. She was halfway to her front door before she heard the car gliding away from the curb.

As she let herself in the front door, the click of the key seemed as loud as a thunderclap, and her own heartbeat echoing in her ears sounded like the thudding of a herd of elephants. *At any second, my parents will wake up and catch me sneaking in,* she thought as she tiptoed up the stairs, cringing at every creak of the wood. But no one stirred, and after what seemed like hours, she was undressed and in bed, the tension oozing out of her sore muscles.

What a night, she thought after looking at

the clock and seeing it was just half past one. Days might have passed since she'd left her room.

So much had happened. She couldn't get over the change in Tony. Had he meant what he'd said about wanting to ask her out? And if he'd meant it, how come he'd sounded so mad? Could he actually think she was so shallow that she'd have turned down a date with him just because he wasn't somebody like Dex?

And who did he think he was, lecturing her on how she should treat her parents?

She tossed and turned for ages before she finally fell asleep, confused thoughts whirling through her mind. If she hadn't felt so close to tears, she might have laughed. To think how desperately she'd wanted to date when she hadn't been allowed to! Now, she was starting to think the whole dating thing was more trouble than it was worth. So far, dating and boys in general had caused her nothing but aggravation.

EIGHTEEN

Gina was astonished when she found Dex waiting by her locker in the morning, his handsome face grim and worried.

"What happened to you last night?" he asked anxiously. "You didn't really think I wasn't going to take you home, did you?"

"Why do you care?" she asked coolly. "You got to stay and have a good time. Isn't that all that mattered?"

"Hey, come on, Gina, don't be like that," he pleaded. "I was just kidding around. I thought you were just playing hard to get. I'd have taken you home eventually."

"You're all heart," she said dryly, putting her jacket in her locker and reaching in for her books.

"Look, I'm sorry. I hardly slept all night, I was so worried. I would have called you first thing this morning, but I was sure you'd just hang up on me."

"I probably would have," she told him bluntly.

"Hey, I said I'm sorry, didn't I?" he asked, with a touch of his usual spirit. "Let's just forget the whole thing happened, all right? I'll never do anything like that again."

"Why did you do it, Dex?" She turned to face him. "Why did you lie to get me to go out there with you?"

He shrugged. "You know how it is. My brother's always showing off his dates, so I didn't want to show up without a date. I wanted Mark to see how neat *my* girlfriend was."

Gina shook her head, smiling to herself. It had never occurred to her that Dex might be just as obsessed with what other people thought as she'd been. "All right, Dex," she said evenly. "We'll forget the whole thing ever happened."

"Friends?" he asked gently, smiling in the way she'd always found devastating. Oddly enough, it now struck her as calculated.

"Friends," she agreed.

"We still going to Mary's party after the game?"

She nodded. "Sure, why not? As long as you promise no funny stuff from now on."

"Promise." He made a big thing of crossing his heart. "From now on, babe, you're the boss."

She headed for homeroom wondering why she wasn't feeling more satisfied and triumphant. *You won, didn't you?* she told herself. *Now you have Dex right where you want him. You can have him on your own terms.*

But she wasn't so sure she wanted him, after all.

All day, she couldn't stop thinking about Tony. She remembered the way he'd looked at her in his car the night before, and it was as if she'd never really looked at him before. If she had, surely she'd have noticed how his eyelashes were so long and silky they almost brushed his cheeks when his eyes were closed, or how his dark hair curled behind his ears, or how lean and powerful his torso was. *Maybe Tony was right,* she thought. *I looked at him and saw only a boy my parents approved of.*

And I looked at Dex and saw the all-American boy. But did I ever look past Dex's exterior? Did I ever think about what Dex was like, instead of what Dex looked like? And, just as important, did I let him know what I'm like, what I really want or care about? When she considered it, it wasn't surprising that Dex had expected her to do whatever he wanted.

Well, from now on things will be different with Dex, she told herself as she settled into her homeroom seat.

But the thing that was most different, she realized as the day wore on, was the way she was feeling. Instead of feeling smug because she'd scored points with Dex, Gina found herself feeling unaccountably glum, as if she'd lost something important.

In history class, as she glanced across the room at Dex, stretched out in his usual sprawl as he doodled in his notebook, she realized that the events of Brinton's Lake had already begun to fade, to seem like the memory of a bad dream. And the anger and defensiveness she'd felt toward Tony had disappeared. As she thought about it now, she had to admit that he'd been right about a lot of things.

Her folks, for one thing.

She didn't think for a minute that they were capable of changing as Tony had insisted. They'd never fit in, not really. But she was starting to see that this was a poor excuse for treating them the way she did. She had shut them out of her life for fear that the really slick sophisticated kids like Dex would laugh at them. If Tony was right, she'd hurt them by doing so.

Doggedly, she tried to concentrate on the

class discussion, but the same thought kept coming back into her mind. *I should invite my folks to come and watch me cheer at this week's game.* She knew she should at least make the gesture to include them in her activities.

She looked at Dex again. Today he wore the red sweater she was crazy about, with soft camel-colored cords and a pair of Frye boots. He looked gorgeous as ever, and Gina's pulse quickened automatically. He was so darned irresistible in some ways! *But that doesn't mean he's the guy for you,* she told herself. By the time the bell rang at the end of class she knew what she had to do.

Gina gathered up her things but stayed by her desk, not making an effort to hide the fact that she was waiting for Dex.

When he spotted her waiting, he made sure he took his own sweet time in coming over, and Gina knew she'd have been a fool to think she'd ever have the upper hand in this relationship. Power meant a lot to a boy like Dex, who was already mapping out his future like a series of chess moves. And Gina didn't doubt that whenever he lost ground in a romance, he'd make sure he gained it back, with more to boot.

"What's up, babe?" he asked as he came up to her, but his smile and raised eyebrows indicated it was only natural a girl would want to spend every possible minute close to his side.

"I just wanted to talk to you for a second," she said lightly.

"You're not still mad about last night, are you?" he asked. "Don't worry"—he lowered his voice—"I didn't tell anybody you were there."

She almost laughed out loud. Leave it to Dex to trick her into sneaking out at night and then assure her he was keeping her secret to protect her reputation! "I said that's all over and done with, and I meant it," Gina assured him. "Only, I think maybe we should stop seeing each other, Dex. At least for a while."

His jaw dropped, and for the first time ever, Gina got to see the silver-tongued Dex Grantham at a loss for words. "What are you talking about?" he finally blurted. "You say you're not mad, then you tell me you don't want to see me anymore? Is this a joke or something?"

She shook her head. "I'm not mad, and I do want to be friends. But I just don't think we're cut out for each other, Dex."

"Are you serious?" His eyes flashed and a vein running along the underside of his chin and down his neck throbbed as he argued, "How can you say that? We're the best dancers in the school, for one thing. We're a great couple! You've got to be kidding."

"We're two great people. Only, not together," she insisted, keeping her tone easy. It was difficult to conceal her amazement that, after all this time of wanting to be by Dex's side, she was the one saying that they should break up. Another part of her wanted to smile at his words. Imagine thinking that just because they both danced well they made a good couple!

Dex opened up his mouth as if to protest again. Then he closed it and smiled. Gina wasn't especially surprised when he finally just shrugged casually. Dex Grantham was going to go through life acting cool if it killed him. "If that's how you want it, babe," he said, his voice soft but nonchalant, his shrug indicating there were plenty of other fish in the sea. "Just let me know if you ever change your mind." He winked, then hurried away. Dex clearly wasn't cut out for good-byes.

Gina walked to her locker with a feeling of relief. She knew she wouldn't get Dex completely out of her system overnight, and part of her was mentally kicking herself already for letting him go. But she knew deep down inside he wasn't the boy who'd make her happy.

Was Tony Genovese that boy?

Gina didn't know for sure. She just knew she wanted to find out. She pulled on her jacket and scooped up her books, then hurried toward the parking lot door to try to find Tess and a ride home. She hoped it wasn't too late to show Tony she'd finally come to her senses.

NINETEEN

The Midvale High School gym was filled to the rafters, and those rafters were shaking now as the home fans counted and stomped out the remaining seconds left in the second quarter. "Ten . . . nine . . . eight . . . seven . . ."

For about the fiftieth time that night, Gina looked up high to where her folks and Tony were on their feet, adding their voices to the countdown. Little Dino stood on the bleacher above his father, grasping his shoulders for support, his face contorted with the excitement of rooting for the home team.

Gina had been surprised at how eagerly her parents had accepted her invitation to come to the game. She'd felt like a louse, and their enthusiasm had just made it worse. It wasn't just because she'd never asked them before—it was because she'd invited them more for Tony's sake than for her own.

It was her way of showing him she was willing to change. Then, too, when she'd phoned him the other day after school, she was afraid he'd say no if she invited him alone. This way, it didn't seem so much like a date, even though she made sure he knew she wouldn't be with Dex. "Mama and Dad and Dino are coming to this weekend's game," she'd told him, her heart in her throat, "and I wanted to invite you to come, too. I—I don't have a date, so we could go out for a Coke afterward. Or even to this party I was invited to."

There was such a long pause, she'd almost hung up, afraid he was going to tell her to get lost. When he'd finally said, "Thanks, Gina, I'd like that a lot," she could have shouted with joy.

Tony had parked his car at her house, so the whole group would arrive together, but Gina had been picked up earlier by Tess, so she didn't get a chance to see him until she and Stacy had led the rest of the squad out onto the floor. Then, glad they were starting out with a cheer that didn't require a lot of concentration, she'd let her eyes rake the stands searching for him.

When she spotted him, her heart lodged

somewhere in her throat. It was as if she'd never noticed before how downright adorable he was.

Next to him sat her parents, and at first Gina was aware only that they *did* look a little out of place. Her mother had put on the casual slacks and sweater Gina had suggested she wear, but her dressy fur-collared coat was draped over her shoulders, while her father had removed his jacket so that his suspenders were in full view as he wildly waved his Midvale pennant, cheering all the while. Dino bounced up and down in his seat, as at home here as he was every place he went.

But what struck her next was how happy and comfortable her mother and father looked here. They didn't seem to feel out of place, and that was what mattered. When Gina caught Tony's eye and he smiled, she knew she'd done the right thing.

She glanced up again in the middle of a jump, and tears blurred her vision. Her parents' faces were lit with pride for her. At that moment she knew she'd do anything she could to show them how much she loved them both.

When all the cheerleaders headed for the locker room during the half, Gina braced herself for a little teasing about her parents' enthusiasm.

"Your folks look like they're having the time of their lives," Tess told her cheerfully. "I can't believe they never bothered coming to the games before when they like basketball so much. We should have your father at all our pep rallies."

That wasn't so bad, Gina thought. Aloud, she said, "Oh, they'll be coming more often from now on."

"And who's that cute guy sitting with them?" Stacy chimed in. "Isn't that the one who took you to last year's prom?"

Gina nodded. "Tony. You really think he's cute?"

"He's adorable!" Stacy said. She wrinkled her nose. "And a big improvement over Dex. You know, I never could believe you were going out with him. I'm glad you finally saw what a waste he is."

"You couldn't believe *I* went out with him? But, Stacy, you went out with him yourself!"

Gina was surprised to see Stacy Harcourt blushing. "Don't rub it in," she said lightly. "Dex is definitely good-looking. But I'd never have dated him more than once if I wasn't feeling so insecure after Nick broke up with me. And Dex really knew how to get to me, too! He was always criticizing me, little things, you know?

He'd say, wasn't my hair getting a little too long, or didn't I think my eye shadow was a little flashy? He'd almost convinced me that I needed him to make me popular again, that I was lucky to be seeing him!"

"Yeah, I can imagine him saying things like that," Gina admitted wryly.

"Thank goodness I came to my senses before he'd completely destroyed any confidence I had left!" Stacy said thankfully.

"You mean *you* dumped *him?*" she asked.

"Sure," Stacy said matter-of-factly. "Why, did he tell you I was the ditchee and he was the ditcher? I'm not surprised. You know, Dex is probably more insecure than all the rest of us put together. I don't suppose he could ever admit somebody didn't want him."

"Tess," Gina said slowly, "when you said, a long time ago, that you didn't think Dex was my type, you meant it, didn't you?"

"I wouldn't have said it if I hadn't meant it," Tess answered calmly. "I always thought you deserved a more sensitive guy. I think Dex is funny and all that, but not serious boyfriend material."

"But he's so great-looking!" Gina couldn't stop shaking her head. "I'd think any girl would be dying to go out with him."

"Maybe—if looks were everything. Then I'd be panting after some cretin like Howie Fellows instead of being happy with a nice guy like Dave. And Stacy would probably still be seeing Dex and not even knowing Jeremy was alive."

"Mmm," Stacy agreed. "But I refuse to believe I wouldn't have fallen for Jeremy, no matter what."

"You know," Gina said thoughtfully, "I'm glad I got a chance to go out with Dex, even if it was just to find out what really matters in a guy."

"Stick with Tony," Stacy advised her. "He looks like a winner to me."

"I think I'm going to try to do that if I haven't blown it already," she admitted with a smile, feeling closer to Stacy than ever before.

"Ready to head back to the gym?" Stacy asked.

"You go ahead," Gina said. "I'll be right out."

When she was alone in the locker room, she took a good, long look at herself in the mirror. *I was wrong about a lot of things,* she thought, *willing to jump to the wrong conclusion, even if it meant ignoring my own best judgment. I was wrong when I thought everyone figured Dex was too good a catch for me. I was wrong when I assumed people were friendlier once I started dating Dex.* It occurred to her as she gazed in the mirror that those people may have been responding to real changes in her behavior. Once Dex had asked her out, she'd felt more acceptable, more confident. That had made her friendlier. Her own shyness had built a wall between her and her friends.

Now that that wall was down, Gina was determined not to let it appear again. She would invite kids to her house. She'd introduce them to her parents. They weren't like all the other parents in Midvale, but they cared about her as much as any parents could, and that was what mattered most. After the game, she would introduce them to Ms. Bowen. Eventually, she might ask the cheering coach to help her talk to her parents about studying dance again. Suddenly Gina felt that nothing was impossible.

But all that can wait, she thought, taking one last look in the mirror before she left the locker room. In the meantime, she had the whole second half of the game to get through. And when it was over, Tony would be coming back home with Gina and her parents.

It was too soon to know what was going to happen with her and Tony. She had acted so stupidly and flaunted her stupidity in front of him. But she couldn't stop hoping. After all, she and Tony had a lot in common. They were both

Italian, and they were both as American as apple pie, too. And Gina had a feeling they were going to find all sorts of other things to share.

With a quick, happy smile for Tony and her parents, she ran back into the gym to do what she did best. All of a sudden, Gina Damone had a lot to cheer about.

WINNERS
by Suzanne Rand

Great new Sweet Dreams mini-series

Being seventeen can be great—and it can be hell! So Stacy Harcourt, Gina Damone and Tess Belding discover as they enter their exciting senior year at Midvale High School. Apart from years of friendship, the popular trio share their main interests in common—an obsession with cheerleading in the elite school squad—and boys! Each book in the series highlights one of the girls, each of whom are from very different backgrounds and families.

Available now

17261 1 THE GIRL MOST LIKELY
17262 X ALL AMERICAN GIRL

Forthcoming

17263 0 CAREER GIRL

Available wherever Bantam paperbacks are sold.

20323 1 P.S. I LOVE YOU (1) *Barbara Conklin*
20325 8 THE POPULARITY PLAN (2) *Rosemary Vernon*
20327 4 LAURIE'S SONG (3) *Suzanne Rand*
20328 2 PRINCESS AMY (4) *Melinda Pollowitz*
20326 6 LITTLE SISTER (5) *Yvonne Greene*
20324 X CALIFORNIA GIRL (6) *Janet Quin-Harkin*
20604 4 GREEN EYES (7) *Suzanne Rand*
20601 X THE THOROUGHBRED (8) *Joanna Campbell*
20744 X COVER GIRL (9) *Yvonne Greene*
20745 8 LOVE MATCH (10) *Janet Quin-Harkin*
20787 3 THE PROBLEM WITH LOVE (11) *Rosemary Vernon*
20788 1 NIGHT OF THE PROM (12) *Debra Spector*
17779 6 THE SUMMER JENNY FELL IN LOVE (13) *Barbara Conklin*
17780 X DANCE OF LOVE (14) *Jocelyn Saal*
17781 8 THINKING OF YOU (15) *Jeanette Nobile*
17782 6 HOW DO YOU SAY GOODBYE? (16) *Margaret Burman*
17783 4 ASK ANNIE (17) *Suzanne Rand*
17784 2 TEN BOY SUMMER (18) *Janet Quin-Harkin*
17791 5 LOVE SONG (19) *Anne Park*
17792 3 THE POPULARITY SUMMER (20) *Rosemary Vernon*
17793 1 ALL'S FAIR IN LOVE (21) *Jeanne Andrews*
17794 X SECRET IDENTITY (22) *Joanna Campbell*
17797 4 FALLING IN LOVE AGAIN (23) *Barbara Conklin*
17800 8 THE TROUBLE WITH CHARLIE (24) *Jay Ellen*
17795 8 HER SECRET SELF (25) *Rhondi Vilott*
17796 6 IT MUST BE MAGIC (26) *Marian Woodruff*
17798 2 TOO YOUNG FOR LOVE (27) *Gailanne Maravel*
17801 6 TRUSTING HEARTS (28) *Jocelyn Saal*
17813 X NEVER LOVE A COWBOY (29) *Jesse Dukore*
17814 8 LITTLE WHITE LIES (30) *Lois I. Fisher*
17839 3 TOO CLOSE FOR COMFORT (31) *Debra Spector*
17840 7 DAYDREAMER (32) *Janet Quin-Harkin*
17841 5 DEAR AMANDA (33) *Rosemary Vernon*
17842 3 COUNTRY GIRL (34) *Melinda Pollowitz*
17843 1 FORBIDDEN LOVE (35) *Marian Woodruff*
17844 X SUMMER DREAMS (36) *Barbara Conklin*
17846 6 PORTRAIT OF LOVE (37) *Jeanette Nobile*
17847 4 RUNNING MATES (38) *Jocelyn Saal*
17848 2 FIRST LOVE (39) *Debra Spector*
17849 0 SECRETS (40) *Anna Aaron*
17850 4 THE TRUTH ABOUT ME AND BOBBY V (41) *Janetta Johns*
17851 2 THE PERFECT MATCH (42) *Marian Woodruff*
17850 2 TENDER LOVING CARE (43) *Anne Park*
17853 9 LONG DISTANCE LOVE (44) *Jesse Dukore*
17069 4 DREAM PROM (45) *Margaret Burman*
17070 8 ON THIN ICE (46) *Jocelyn Saal*
17071 6 TE AMO MEANS I LOVE YOU (47) *Deborah Kent*

17072 4	DIAL L FOR LOVE (48)	*Marian Woodruff*
17073 2	TOO MUCH TO LOSE (49)	*Suzanne Rand*
17074 0	LIGHTS, CAMERA, LOVE (50)	*Gailanne Maravel*
17075 9	MAGIC MOMENTS (51)	*Debra Spector*
17076 7	LOVE NOTES (52)	*Joanna Campbell*
17087 2	GHOST OF A CHANCE (53)	*Janet Quin-Harkin*
17088 0	I CAN'T FORGET YOU (54)	*Lois I. Fisher*
17089 9	SPOTLIGHT ON LOVE (55)	*Nancy Pines*
17090 2	CAMPFIRE NIGHTS (56)	*Dale Novack*
17871 7	ON HER OWN (57)	*Suzanne Rand*
17872 5	RHYTHM OF LOVE (58)	*Stephanie Foster*
17873 3	PLEASE SAY YES (59)	*Alice Owen Crawford*
17874 1	SUMMER BREEZES (60)	*Susan Blake*
17875 X	EXCHANGE OF HEARTS (61)	*Janet Quin-Harkin*
17876 8	JUST LIKE THE MOVIES (62)	*Suzanne Rand*
24150 8	KISS ME, CREEP (63)	*Marian Woodruff*
24151 6	LOVE IN THE FAST LANE (64)	*Rosemary Vernon*
24152 4	THE TWO OF US (65)	*Janet Quin-Harkin*
24153 2	LOVE TIMES TWO (66)	*Stephanie Foster*
24180 X	I BELIEVE IN YOU (67)	*Barbara Conklin*
24181 8	LOVEBIRDS (68)	*Janet Quin-Harkin*
24254 7	CALL ME BEAUTIFUL (69)	*Shannon Blair*
24255 5	SPECIAL SOMEONE (70)	*Terri Fields*
24355 1	TOO MANY BOYS (71)	*Celia Dickenson*
24356 X	GOODBYE FOREVER (72)	*Barbara Conklin*
24357 8	LANGUAGE OF LOVE (73)	*Rosemary Vernon*
24381 0	DON'T FORGET ME (74)	*Diana Gregory*
24382 9	FIRST SUMMER LOVE (75)	*Stephanie Foster*
24385 3	THREE CHEERS FOR LOVE (76)	*Suzanne Rand*
24387 X	TEN-SPEED SUMMER (77)	*Deborah Kent*
24384 5	NEVER SAY NO (78)	*Jean F. Capron*
24971 1	STAR STRUCK (79)	*Shannon Blair*
24386 1	A SHOT AT LOVE (80)	*Jill Jarnow*
24688 7	SECRET ADMIRER (81)	*Debra Spector*
24383 7	HEY, GOOD LOOKING! (82)	*Jane Polcovar*
24823 5	LOVE BY THE BOOK (83)	*Anne Park*
24718 2	THE LAST WORD (84)	*Susan Blake*
24890 1	THE BOY SHE LEFT BEHIND (85)	*Suzanne Rand*
24945 2	QUESTIONS OF LOVE (86)	*Rosemary Vernon*
24824 3	PROGRAMMED FOR LOVE (87)	*Marion Crane*
24891 X	WRONG KIND OF BOY (88)	*Shannon Blair*
24946 0	101 WAYS TO MEET MR RIGHT (89)	*Janet Quin-Harkin*
24992 4	TWO'S A CROWD (90)	*Diana Gregory*
25070 1	THE LOVE HUNT (91)	*Yvonne Greene*
25131 7	KISS AND TELL (92)	*Shannon Blair*
25071 X	THE GREAT BOY CHASE (93)	*Janet Quin-Harkin*
25132 5	SECOND CHANCES (94)	*Nancy Levinson*
25178 3	NO STRINGS ATTACHED (95)	*Eileen Hehl*
25179 1	FIRST, LAST, AND ALWAYS (96)	*Barbara Conklin*
25244 5	DANCING IN THE DARK (97)	*Carolyn Ross*
25245 3	LOVE IN THE AIR (98)	*Diana Gregory*
25297 6	ONE BOY TOO MANY (99)	*Marian Caudell*
25298 4	FOLLOW THAT BOY (100)	*Debra Spector*
25366 2	WRONG FOR EACH OTHER (101)	*Janet Quin-Harkin*
25367 0	HEARTS DON'T LIE (102)	*Terri Fields*
25428 6	CROSS MY HEART (103)	*Janice Stevens*
25429 4	PLAYING FOR KEEPS (104)	*Diana Gregory*
25469 3	THE PERFECT BOY (105)	*Elizabeth Reynolds*
25470 7	MISSION: LOVE (106)	*Kathryn Makris*
25535 5	IF YOU LOVE ME (107)	*Barbara Steiner*
25536 3	ONE OF THE BOYS (108)	*Jill Jarnow*
25643 2	NO MORE BOYS (109)	*Charlotte White*
256424 4	PLAYING GAMES (110)	*Eileen Hehl*

COUPLES
by Linda A. Cooney

What every girl wants most of all . . . to be part of a *couple.*

No 1: CHANGE OF HEARTS

Meet the couples and couples-to-be of this thrilling new series: pretty Chris and athletic Ted, who are having their problems . . . popular Phoebe, her serious boyfriend Brad, and Griffin, the dreamy actor who threatens their two-year relationship . . . plain Janie and vampy Laurie, who both covet cool D.J. Peter . . . sensitive, artistic Woody, whose love for Phoebe can never be realised . . . and Chris's troubled, troublesome stepsister, Brenda.

0 553 17228X

No 2: FIRE AND ICE

They're as different as night and day! He's the red-hot D.J. of Kennedy High's radio station, at the very pulse of the school's social scene. She's a cool, disciplined iceskater, too busy training to enjoy old friends or school activities. They're the two people least likely to fall in love. Right?

Wrong! Unexpected circumstances throw them together, and Lisa and Peter discover that they may be made for each other after all.

0 553 172298

Also available

0 553 172433 3 ALONE TOGETHER
0 553 172549 4 MADE FOR EACH OTHER
0 553 172662 5 MOVING TOO FAST
0 553 172670 6 CRAZY LOVE

Created by Francine Pascal
Written by Joanna Campbell

From Francine Pascal, creator of SWEET VALLEY HIGH, comes her most irresistibly dazzling star—CAITLIN! She's breathtaking, captivating, outrageous and *unforgettable!*

Book One: CAITLIN: LOVING
To everyone at her exclusive Virginia boarding school, Caitlin seems to have it all. But there is a secret need that haunts her life. A need for love. And only one boy can make her forget her cold home life, can fulfill her need for love: handsome, sensitive Jed Michaels. Jed, who has already given his heart to another girl.

Book Two: CAITLIN: LOVE LOST
Find out what happens when the boy she loves uncovers Caitlin's darkest secret. Can their love survive!

Book Three: CAITLIN: TRUE LOVE
And cross your fingers for Caitlin and Jed when they face a deadly danger. Can *they* survive?

CAITLIN. THERE'S NEVER BEEN A HEROINE LIKE HER!